Saving Mina

Saving Mina

Helen Elizabeth

For my children, Megan, Elliot, and Ruby.

Table of Contents

THE PROLOGUE

Should she hurt him in some way? Make him pay for this pain and loneliness? Wake him sharply, by turning up the lights clinically bright? Knock the scalding coffee she has just made him, across his flaccid groin? Or quietly stick the kitchen knife she is holding in her dressing gown pocket, straight through his rib cage into the middle of his shriveled heart? She breathed in and out, deliberately slowly, gripping the smooth steel tighter. How had it had come to this? She looked across at his nodding head; the rounded shoulders collapsed forward, the troubled breathing. Using the TV remote, she pushed up and down on the volume control, hoping to wake him or at least drown out his deep, rhythmic snoring. Nothing. The intermittent grunting continued. She stroked the blade. She felt uncontrollable, spiteful anger. Night after tedious night, she sat here alone, watching a film of his choosing together. Night after night, she listened to his lies and delusions. Night after night, she listened to the cacophony of his nasal noises, grunts, and

1

shudders. She felt utterly forlorn. She took deep gulps of the wine she was drinking, hoping to steady her nerves. The cat, old and skeletal, gazed lovingly at her through tired eyes. Its ability to purr long gone, they held their gaze briefly, until it closed its eyes listlessly. Flicking, she raced up and down the channels, looking for anything that would take her from this lonely place and time; a medical drama, some new-born infant squeezing its way into the world in a flurry of blood and fluids, a child with an intolerable affliction in an unknown place, innocent young girls with acid wounds or rape stories. These were her nights. Before she knows it, she is crying, big, gulping, self-pitying, silent tears. Grieving for the soft tingle of loving fingertips and delicate lips on naked skin. Her silent grief is overshadowed by the continuing sounds of deep guttural reverberations as his heavy head squashes further into his neck, the mouth open, moist spit in the corner of his mouth. She feels foolish, numb and increasingly old. Deep inside she can hear her youthful self, full of passion and yearning, screaming to get out. She begs for freedom, but she cannot be released, must not be released, must be kept in her shackles in case she fights or flies. She can feel the cold metal in her fist. She rises and stands motionless in front of him. Their coupling reflected in the large mirror above the fireplace. She has no idea who that woman in the mirror is, the one with the delicate wrinkles by her eyes and a neck increasingly not her own. Silently and slowly, she kneels in front of him, watching him in his solitude of sleep – dreaming deeply - another world she has no part in. She watches him intently, the familiar lashes, soft skin permeated with sprouting hair, the lips roughly exhaling air. Suddenly there is silence. No sound, no movement. An absence. She stares at his motionless face, and she too holds her breath; waits…waits…hoping. A clock somewhere ticking, competing, methodical. Then a physical sudden jolt breaks the silence, and she shrinks backwards away from him. The noise begins again, louder, and more persistent, stubbornly eager to keep him alive. She imagines the bigger world, the one she had scoped for herself as a teenager reading French authors, Collette and Simone de Beauvoir. A world of Parisian men and revolutions: drinking wine on tree-lined boulevards, before retiring to smoke-filled attic apartments and afternoons of nakedness and sex. That was the world of fiction and fairy tales she immersed herself in and yearns for now. But what of her plan B? The one she set out to achieve. The one she pursued and fought for? The one she thought she had won. What happened to that? Quietly she stands, resolved. Placing the knife down, she quietly closes the door on him and begins her preparations.

1 THE HAT

It had started with a hat. A big, bold, beautiful hat. Mina had been ambling absent-mindedly through the store when she saw it and knew she had to own it. She didn't even consider the price tag, knew that the cost, half a month's rent, would somehow pay for itself. Knew that this object of beauty was somehow part of her future. She carefully lifted it down and placed it on her head, pulling her dark hair away from her face. The wide, ebony brim accentuated the pallor of her skin and allowed her dark eyes to peep coyly from beneath. As a child she'd felt awkward and ungainly, long spindly legs, knees constantly scabbed from tripping over, skin blighted by acne. She had sought refuge with the beautiful children and as a result, carried the scars of their revulsion. They'd dappled cruelly in her loyalty to them, and her torment had been great. They were petite, with heart-shaped pale faces, blue eyed. She longed for their pretty compactness; curled her shoulders, looked inward, took their brutality gratefully, happy for any attention. She gazed at herself in the hat for a long time, turning her head, lifting her chin, turning her head again, gently touching her cool, now smooth skin. An involuntary smile evolved secretly, unseen by the flurry of alert and purposeful shoppers. She felt a tightening in her belly, guilty of her growing fondness for the woman she was growing into. She was oblivious to the fluorescent lights and the painted woman watching her suspiciously. The hat sat coquettishly, framing her face, a protective amour from the expected criticisms. She knew she had to have it.

'Do you need any help?' She stopped and turned, jolted by the invasion of her contemplations. The assistant's red stained smile and unfriendly eyes indicated towards the hat. 'Only, if you need some help, I have been trained to advise on items such as that.' Again, her frozen face nodded upwards towards Mina, the smile transfixed.

'No. Thank you'. A brisk walk to the till and Mina was pushing in the plastic, punching the numbers, and refusing to think about the remaining three weeks of the month or how she would feed herself. The mundanity of daily life seemed inappropriate, devoid of manners. She would manage.

Outside the shop, hatbox in hand, she walked with purpose, a smile of pride and pleasure as she straightened her back and lifted her head high. She felt like a wealthy princess, or an empress, a stream of servants following dutifully behind. She was powerful and mysterious, far above those living ordinary, ugly lives. She'd been there and done that and wasn't going back. The hat box, large, pink, and cumbersome, swung forward and back on its pretty cord handle, announcing itself to the world. Mina felt a swagger in her walk and went with it. People moved out of her way, and she didn't feel the need to thank them. Sweeping through the crowds she knew her life would change soon. This hat would be her ticket out of here, the start of her future, a world devoid of tedium, early mornings, and mindless chat.

The tube ride home was riddled with complications. She'd contemplated a taxi – demeaning for her 'regal' state of mind - and even more so when you didn't have the cash to pay at the end. Instead, she sat tall, caressing the box close to her chest, and avoided thinking about the addict twitching on the seat next to her. She knew he couldn't be allowed to touch the box, infest it with his lack of ambition, destroy her dream. She wanted it pristine and untouched. He coughed gutturally, and she turned her back away from him, nurturing the box closer to her chest, preventing any contagion, counting down the station stops to her own.

For days, the hat box sat in pride of place on the kitchen table. Every evening she sat and marked her students' books, careful always not to infect the box with their futile feelings of teenage romance and celebrity. Their lack of depth was astonishing. They appeared to lack any sense of beauty, of love and of poetry. They understood the world of virtual TV and celebrity, of boob jobs, of fake tans and bitching. They could barely string a sentence together, couldn't use a capital letter or full stop in the right place, but could spell Louis Vuitton correctly. She muddled through each soiled page, attempting to discern between the monotony of their pubescent attempts. They couldn't be allowed to slur the true beauty of her hat and the untold possibilities it offered, with their fake and borrowed ideas.

Within a week, the food in the fridge became sparse. Up to her overdraft limit, her credit cards maxed and a particularly ungenerous mother, she gathered invites to friends and volunteered for extra lunch duties at school. Living alone, Mina's lack of food went unnoticed by her work mates and close friends. She arrived bright and awake every morning in the staffroom, drinking copious amounts of tea and dunking the odd biscuit. There was no threat of her starving and in fact, she felt slightly trimmer around the waist. At night, opening the door to her tiny flat, any pangs of hunger disappeared as she saw the imposing box sat where a plate of food should be.

Finally, one joyous Saturday morning, following a gifted bottle of wine and subsequent intoxicated sleep, Mina's plan B began to take shape. Still a week until payday, she was beginning to wonder whether she would have to destroy all moral integrity and make the begging phone call home. On the last few teabags and having had only a handful of meal offers over the last week, Mina was beginning to feel hungry. Several times, she'd dialled the number and then hung up, not prepared to admit to spending a large percentage of her salary on a hat. It had a purpose, she knew it had, she just couldn't decide at that moment what that purpose was. Her mother was a woman who dealt with the practicalities of life, not the beauty. She believed that the world had dealt her a multitude of bad luck, one of them being Mina, who had obviously prevented her from being wealthy and consequently, living life as she expected to live it. Mina repeatedly disappointed, daughters have a habit of doing that, even college graduates, particularly those sullying their hands by teaching teenagers on a tough housing estate in East London. The thought of Mina asking for help was preposterous – inconceivable – why give ammunition to someone who you knew would come back to destroy you? Who would do that? So, a phone call home was out of the question. She remembered a particular teenage night, where she'd dabbled in some speed and woken at 4am with her heart jumping wildly. She had accepted the fact that it was far safer to remain in bed and die of a heart attack than admit to her mother what she'd done. Somehow, she'd managed to survive college and the first year of teaching without asking for a penny, she wasn't going to start now over a slight, shortage in the food department. So, when she climbed out of bed on that brutally cold March morning and saw the elegant handwriting on the envelope, she knew the moment had arrived. It was a wedding invitation. An invitation to a society wedding of a lone school friend Mina had long since lost touch with. She marvelled that she'd been thought of and only slightly grieved over the fact that the invite was for her alone. Then she thought about the hat, sat patiently waiting its time, this surely was it. She smiled to herself and set the elegant invitation in pride of place, next to the hat box.

2 THE WEDDING INVITATION

Mina picked up the phone and dialed. It had been a while since she'd spoken to Lucy, over a year, a friendship that had been postponed rather than ended. Lucy's romance had been a surprise, even to Mina who was used to the rest of the world finding their soul mates on a constant and sporadic basis. She'd heard through mutual friends that Lucy had been dating a fellow medical student and that they'd become inseparable. What she didn't know was that they'd traversed a snowy mountain, taken in some French air and then he'd placed a solid rock on her meaningful finger. Lucy had known since a small child, that her footsteps would follow that of her surgeon father. She was determined, resilient and fascinatingly bright. This romance and now wedding, felt decidedly like a detour to Mina, a cul-de-sac that might stall this well-bred woman. The dial tone was replaced by a particularly happy message from Lucy, proclaiming her absence and suggesting a message be left.

'Hi Lucy. Umm just to say...well congratulations!' Mina stopped, conscious of a ticking as the answer phone waited patiently for her message, 'So happy for you…you must be thrilled'. Did she really just say that? No wonder her friendship group could be counted on one hand. 'Thanks for the invite. I'd love to come. Well…umm…yep…bye.'

She put the phone down and sat still, amazed by the quiet of her flat. Lucy had sounded so jubilant, so invigorating, so different to the Lucy she'd known at school. That Lucy studied hard and was sensible. That Lucy hadn't dappled in boyfriends, drugs, or dancing. This Lucy sounded like she was doing all three and the effect was hugely intoxicating and alienating at the same time. As girls, they'd sat together in lessons and Mina had found her refreshingly simple. She wasn't part of the beautiful group, choosing instead to keep herself private and alone. She didn't bitch like some of the others, didn't cry or have tantrums. Lucy wasn't a schoolgirl princess, she was straightforward and consequently, often a little dull. Mina wanted to be popular and liked. Lucy didn't care or didn't seem to. Consequently, in her darkest moments, Mina found herself seeking refuge in the library, where inevitably Lucy would be. Gradually they had assumed an understanding – shared the same space – talked about their work and their aspirations.

Mina turned the invitation over in her hand. The embossed card was understated and loudly proclaimed the quality of both its inception and the calibre of wedding. She had six weeks to prepare, six weeks to ensure that plan B became a reality. She wondered who else would have been invited. Other solitary friends? She had to admit, staying in touch with people wasn't her thing, she wasn't committed enough. Social media annoyed her and most of her friends seemed to have left university attached, coupled, organized. She thought about her last dalliance. He had appeared keen, happy to succumb to her sporadic requests and regular dismissals. Finally, she had deliberately applied for a teaching job 120 miles away, to avoid the inevitable let-down conversation, let geography do her talking for her. Lucy, like Mina, had shared this desire for non-committal. Through university they had met up for the odd weekend, shared the odd tale, grumbled about work pressure and male commitment. Yet here she was, betraying their common interests to pledge devotion to a man on a public arena. Mina shuddered quietly, before giving herself a quiet talking to.

3 PRE-WEDDING NERVES

The six weeks leading up to the wedding had been busy. It was exam time in school; mock exams, controlled assessments and marking. Mina filled her evenings plodding through pages of disorganized, uninspiring, and grubby attempts at writing. She'd received a text from Lucy, acknowledging her acceptance of the invitation and apologizing for not having contacted her personally, she'd been very busy, long work hours and a lover!

The hat now had an outfit to accompany it. A simple black dress, tight and a little low, to show off her rather insignificant breasts and her elongated neck. The shoes had been more difficult, red her preferred, seemed too vampy for a Spring wedding. Instead, she opted for a neutral shade that seamlessly added another three inches to her long legs. The whole impression was demure, and she hoped sophisticated and sexy. Going alone was going to be difficult. She'd forced herself to check Facebook, hoping to gauge whether other single friends were going – she was definitely not going to advertise the fact that firstly, she had an invite and secondly, that she was going alone. Instead, she watched and waited, hoping that someone else would have the courage to admit to going alone and then she would have rescued them, offered to accompany them, share a taxi home. But as the weeks passed, it became clear that she was going to have to front it out. Mina had become skilled at this. She practised the art of solo socializing. At times, entering a bar alone and ordering a drink felt empowering and sophisticated. At others, she felt ashamed and vulnerable, mocked and pitied by women her age and preyed on by predatory men. But the worst was the feeling of ostracism. Coupled friends were gradually not inviting her to events. She had no idea why. She wasn't a predatory female, had never made a pass at any of their partners and certainly wasn't interested in an affair. But gradually overtime, less invites came.

A fortnight before the wedding, sat in a particularly loud wine bar with some colleagues, Mina felt a sudden surge of excitement, a glow. The discussion had been tedious, moans about challenging classes, high expectations of senior leaders and the price of rent. When suddenly, Lucy walked through the door, smiling, clean-faced and genuinely excited to see Mina. They'd hugged, kissed and then after quickly introducing her to some of her workmates, Mina dragged her to the bar under the premise of buying her a drink.

'It's so good to see you, Mina. It's been so long. You look incredible.'

'So do you. You look so happy.' She did, radiant.

'I know. Don't ask me what happened. One

minute I'm surviving fifteen-hour days, the next I'm trying on wedding gowns. I'm meeting his sister in a minute; final discussion about flowers and such. I never realized it was so complicated.'

Lucy's excited grin lacked any smugness; pure, self-absorbed contentment. She looked at ease with herself and with the world in general. 'I'm so excited that you can come to the wedding. I haven't forgotten you you know. I have a little plan of my own.' Mina passed Lucy a large glass of Sauvignon Blanc and examined the pennies the bar tender had returned to her.

'Plan? Do I need a plan?' Mina felt slightly resentful, as if being her, necessitated a friend's planning.

'Put it this way.' Lucy stopped and smiled at Mina. 'Simon has some very interesting friends, some very interesting single friends.'

'Thank God for that. I won't be the only one. Was beginning to think I was a rare and not very interesting breed.' She was genuinely relieved, could feel her breathing relax, her heart calming. The chatter around them was relentless and she found herself leaning in closer to catch Lucy's animated tones.

'Now, I have been somewhat creative with the seating plan and sat you between two decidedly gorgeous men. One, is extremely wealthy, ridiculously so. And the other, well, he is particularly charming! My gift to you Mina for all those years you loyally and persistently tried to make me have fun!' Lucy turned as the door opened and a woman waved an acknowledgement across the room. 'Sorry – Simon's sister. Let's catch up properly soon. It's fantastic seeing you. You look so…so well.' Lucy began to turn.

'Hold on! You can't just say that and then go. It's out there now. I need names, details, dos and don'ts!' Mina grabbed Lucy's arm.

'Sorry. Can't. Look you'll love them both. Really – I mean it. Just enjoy Mina! Perhaps we can catch up when we get back – you know – from the honeymoon and stuff. I'll phone. I promise. I'll send you some dates.' Lucy grabbed her close, holding her for a worthy few seconds before grinning girlishly and widely. 'I promise, it's going to be fun.'

Mina watched as Lucy wriggled her way through the crowded room and hugged the stranger who was removing their jacket at the door. She stood quietly. Her head needed to digest the information. Was this some cruel, schoolgirl joke? A way for coupled people to humiliate her in her solitary state. She ordered another and began to visualize these 'interesting' friends, the unknown groom Simon had. She wasn't sure whether what she was feeling was even comfortable – 'my gift to you'. What the hell did that mean? Pity? Friendship? Either could be interpreted. She wasn't even sure now whether she wanted to go, the whole thing was becoming a little too complex. She'd thought, flouncy dresses, champagne, some food, a bit of dancing and some healthy flirting. Now she had a potential millionaire sat one side and a cad the other! All arranged by a school friend who had never been particularly good at judging male qualities. I mean, she hadn't even met this Simon, just seen a few posted pictures of him and Lucy grinning mindlessly at each other over hot chocolate in the Alps.

Re-joining her friends, she listened soberly and politely to their staffroom woes, her mind racing. She smiled at the relevant moments, interjected the odd moan and nodded empathetically. She even managed a couple of appropriate anecdotes to move the conversation on. It was then that the warm glow began to dissipate around her body. She realized that she was blushing, that her heart was actually pounding and that her mind was far away from the noise and clutter of this sweaty bar. The frenetic energy of the bustle began to make her feel claustrophobic. She couldn't hear herself think. She needed to think. She felt slightly woozy and startled the others by suddenly getting up and heading quickly for the exit.

Outside, it was cold, and she turned her face skyward, taking deep gulps of the night air. The sky was clear and sombre.

'Hey, you ok Mina?' Nicole stood beside her, fingertips gently touching her shoulder.

'I'm fine. It's the wine. Didn't have time for lunch. You go back in. I might just head off home.' She smiled confidently, hoping to dissuade further talk.

'You sure?'

'Course. I'll see you in the morning.' Mina forced a wide grin and winked, trying to reassure both herself and Nicole. 'Just need sleep – will be fine in the morning.'

'Really?' Nicole genuinely cared, Mina

understood this and relished her concern. They'd met in their first year of teaching and there was instant attraction. They'd looked across the school hall on the first training morning and knew that they would be friends. Both had exchanged shared glances of fear and awe, neither confident that their career choice was going to be a preferred style. Since then, they had nursed each other through poor decisions, brutal classroom situations, leering middle-aged protagonists leaning on the photocopier and held each other's hair out of alcohol-induced vomit. Most importantly, they were connected but not together, neither needing to feed off the other, respectful of their downtimes. In this way, they had endured a seemingly brief but deep friendship.

'Hey Mina – it's me you are talking to. You sure you're ok? You would tell me?' Mina smiled reassurance. 'If, you are sure?' Nicole continued to hold her gaze. 'Hey Mina. You know where I am, you know that don't you.' The door opened, and Nicole stepped back into the throng of the bar, the rumble of chorused voices blundering briefly, affronting the cool quiet outside. Within seconds, Mina was left alone with the dark sky and the traffic for company.

Later, opening her front door, she felt coldly alone. Switching on the lights in the frosty kitchen, she looked at the hat box sat on the kitchen table and smiled.

4 THE WEDDING

The sun, high in the sky, lit the courtyard where the guests mingled, gossiped, and smiled. It reflected off the champagne flutes, luminescing their faces and causing long, elongated shadows across the cobblestones. Beautiful people strolled aimlessly in its warmth. Some moved in time to the string quartet, some motionless, deep in conversation. A flurry of dresses permeated the black of suits and the odd glimpse of Lucy's ivory frock. Mina stood by the stable bar, was camouflaged amongst the throng of men. She peeped coquettishly from under the brim of her hat, thankful for the protection from the sun's increasingly strong rays and smiled warmly at every passing comment. Wishing she'd not worn long gloves, Mina struggled to pick up the hors d'oeuvres being served on small silver trays and instead, decided another glass of bubbly would be more beneficial. She knew hardly anyone. Was surprised by the lack of friends from their past. Perhaps she was the solitary person Lucy classed as a friend from those days? So instead, she hovered aimlessly, not really sure who to talk to, listening intently and trying to look preoccupied as she clasped the safety of the bar.

The actual wedding in the estate's church, had been traditional and long, the vicar using the ceremony as an excuse to impart his perceived wisdom on a new congregation of supposedly unbelievers. Mina had sat quietly near the back, avoiding the tempting lure of her mobile phone whilst he spoke of the dangers of adultery and the pleasures of giving oneself to another for all eternity. Swans and particular breeds of penguins do that she thought, not humans. Throughout, she'd surveyed the church, attempting to hunt down her prospective 'eligible men' without looking too much like a desperate meerkat. In the end, bells ringing, bridesmaids walking and organ grinding loudly, it was difficult to discern anyone in particular amongst the throng. Instead, she attempted to remain alluring and elegant, as she tackled in heels, the precarious walk on a stone driveway up to the main house.

The drawing room was elegant. Duck egg blue walls, ornate gold and crystal adorning the walls and ceiling. The brisk, white sterile tablecloths were littered with tiny vases of summer blossoms and cutlery bright and polished. Mina walked cautiously through the room, wriggling past those already seated, apologizing if the corner of a hat or shoulder was touched. Ahead, a circular table was filling fast. People politely checking the name cards and swopping chairs as appropriate, a mixture of black and pastels, white teeth, and pleasantries. Mina's heart was racing with both fear and speculation as she reached the table and saw the remaining empty chair. A few people turned their heads, smiled, and said hello. Lowering herself delicately into the empty chair she was conscious of the suit either side of her. Mina was about to introduce herself when the maître D announced the arrival of Mr and Mrs Fallow and the whole room stood.

She wasn't immediately conscious of either man stood beside her. She glimpsed the corner of both their mourning suits and caught a faint waft of something musky amongst the overbearing smell of bridal lilies. She didn't want to start awkward introductions. Instead, she stood with everyone else and clapped the smiling couple as they walked hand in hand across the room and took their place at the bridal table. She knew both men were taller than her, one significantly so. She sensed that one was slightly darker, though again this felt like perception rather than knowledge of the facts. The hat that had protected her from the harsh sun, was now hiding her from the facts she so desperately wanted to gather. It was consuming her face and making her feel hot and slightly pink in the cheeks. She could see their hands, rhythmically clapping, both lean and strong, one slightly hairier than the other. Her own hands, small and polished, trembled as she concentrated on the confirmatory action, smiling and standing still, so that her hat wouldn't involuntarily knock either man. She wished Lucy hadn't told her. Wished she was innocent to any facts about anyone at her table. Wished she wasn't so lonely and somewhat desperate. It was inconceivable to believe that she was using her friend's wedding to obtain a man. And yet, wasn't that what she was intending on doing? Wasn't that the game plan, the plan B? She imagined herself, quietly watching the proceedings from on high, the pantomime playing out below, the outfits, the smiling strangers, the rituals, the performances. The exorbitant display of emotion and materialism. She felt slightly giddy. Wished she'd eaten something before beginning on the champagne. Wished she was back at home with the cat and a cup of tea.

No one spoke as they sat down. The silence was replaced by intense smiling. Any attempt at introductions was marred by a flurry of dishes lifted delicately onto the table. The quartet began, and the cutlery tapped melodically as the guests began to eat. Mina quietly listened to the polite conversation. She realised quickly that this was the table of oddities: friends that the couple knew, but who didn't know each other. She was not alone – they all were! She felt the knot in her stomach begin to dissipate, her breathing slowed, and she felt her shoulders relax. The food kept coming. Little plates emerged and disappeared. Mina wasn't conscious of their contents or her preferences. She listened, she smiled, she ate, and now and again, at an opportune moment she added a comment or two. Nothing more. She was deliberately cautious.

By the end of the speeches, Mina felt full and relaxed. The table conversation had been amicable and light, the speeches suitably brief and amusing and the wine forthcoming. Trapped by her hat, she'd directed most of her conversation across the table and could only listen to the voices of the men either side. She'd kept her elbows suitably in check and other than a glimpse of a chin or a wrist she had no clearer picture of her enforced companions either side of her. It was only when the fading afternoon light precipitated the lighting of some table candles did Mina find the courage to excuse herself from the table. On returning, she found the majority of the room were now roaming free, mingling, ties unfolded, hats removed. Mina moved cautiously, keen not to invade a conversation or appear alone. As she arrived at her table, a head of thick, mousy curls looked up from his phone and beamed.

'Fancy a drink at the bar?' Mina smiled and dutifully followed.

5 DANCING

It was quiet in the woods as they walked, cool and refreshing, a welcome change from the heady, sexual expectation of the dancing. They had danced of course. Smiling and flirting as they moved in and around each other, fingertips touching, hips moving rhythmically, eyes locked. Finally, the music slowing, they had clasped each other, heart beats synchronized, breath against warm necks. Now outside, the cool spring night sobered their consciousness, and the darkness enveloped their embarrassment. They walked in silence. Mina barefoot, tiptoed carefully, conscious of the twigs and earth below her feet. Her hat long gone, she felt naked and dishevelled, her long hair free from its controlled chignon, her dress slightly damp. The trees whispered softly in conspiracy, blocking the bright moon and hiding the nightly prowls of the local creatures. Mina shivered. Daniel stopped and removed his jacket, soberly placing it around her shoulders. She smiled a thank you and they continued. Their fingers found each other in the darkness, first the tips, then the whole hand grasping at each other.

'Do you know where we are going?' Mina whispered.

'Of course. Don't you trust me?' Through the trees, a clearing opened before them. Soft, mossy banks leading down to a wide and fast-moving stream. Briefly they stood and watched. Listened to its noises as it rippled and writhed over debris and low-hanging branches. Watched the moon light the water. Daniel turned to look at her, his dark green eyes searching her face. He reached up and tucked a piece of her hair out of her eyes, stroking her forehead and cheek as he did so, his fingertips delaying next to her mouth. Without a sound, he brought his head close and kissed her, his lips soft and warm, a strong arm holding her tightly in the embrace. She kissed him back, hard and passionate, her head dizzy, the chemistry intense.

'I'm sorry,' he said, 'I shouldn't have.' She stumbled a few steps backwards, breathless, as he let go of his hold.

'It's...it's fine...I...'

'No really, I shouldn't have...you're just so lovely.' She wanted to laugh at this, say something self-deprecating, discard his comment as something trivial, a line. But she didn't. He was looking at her, eyes fixed, sincere. He smiled, creases in the corners of his eyes softening his face. Mina smiled too. He reached up and stroked her hair, her face, his hands finally coming to rest gently on the back of her neck. Their foreheads touched briefly, their breath mingling, eyes engaged. He gently kissed her forehead, then each eye, her cheekbones, his lips barely brushing the skin. Mina was conscious of her breathing, the goosebumps on her skin and her uncontrollable trembling. His lips teased and caressed carefully around her mouth until, taking his face she pulled him close and kissed him hard and urgently. His jacket fell from her shoulders and as one, they followed it down onto the damp grass below. Hands entwined, he spread her arms wide, and she was defenceless to the pressure of his body as he kissed her nape and the top of her breasts. The hoot of an owl broke their spell. They stopped; breathless and silent, their hands still entwined.

Mina lay prostrate in the grass staring up at this stranger's face, smiling. Nothing was said. Quietly they listened to the water as it dipped and dived, oblivious to their stillness. Reluctantly, they let go of their hold and he helped her to her feet.

'Perhaps we should get back to the party. Your poor feet.'

Mina looked down at her stockinged feet and realized that one polished toe was peeping out. She felt a wave of embarrassment.

'I'll take them off when we get back. It's just a little cold at the moment.' The thought of removing stockings in this place felt more than provocative and she wasn't sure she'd be able to undertake the venture sexily.

Hands clasped tightly they walked in silence back to the party. Every now and then, she caught him looking down at her and smiling, which sent warm surges through her body. As the lights of the house came into sight, they stopped and briefly kissed, and he grasped the back of her damp dress hard against his body. She could hear the thumping of the distant music in rhythm with his heartbeat and closed her eyes tight shut. She was conscious of his strong arms, his earthy smell, and the stirrings of a passion unspent. She shivered. Kissing her gently on the top of her head, he silently led her back to the garish gaiety of the wedding party.

6 THE AFTERMATH

The days following the wedding blurred into a continuum of teaching, chores and checking her phone. They had swopped contact details and Mina, loathe to appear too keen or even desperate, had been waiting for his call. She knew very little about him. They'd drunk champagne, danced, walked and kissed. That was it - end of! She was a little surprised that she'd even remembered his name: Daniel. She found herself writing it on post-its, while bored in class, an adolescent inventing her world in different fonts. She'd been cynical of the names she found scribbled on her students' work, daubed unceremoniously on the back of toilet doors, and etched painfully in park benches. Yet here she was absorbed, as if the writing of the name would physically reveal the man.

Years before, she'd fallen for the 'it boy' in class. He was naturally confident, adored by everyone and most importantly, taller than her. For months she had followed him around school, watching his every move from afar. At night, she wrote poems expressing the persistent, personal pain she felt at his dispassion. She felt utterly anguished, the pain in her chest constant. She knew that he had no knowledge of her existence, she was ethereal, something inconsequential. Finally, beside herself, she decided to post him a poem, expressing her true feelings. A few days later, arriving in class, she was met with hoots of laughter, ridicule, and jibes. Her poem had been pinned, naked to the board. They shoved her center stage, blocking the door, while she stood reddened and mortified, as he routinely quoted excerpts. It was a long forty minutes before her escape was assured and she was able to crawl under the study desk and cry uncontrollably. She'd hated him with a passion ever since.

Now, as each hour passed, she became increasingly absorbed, increasingly angry. She trawled social networking sites, looking for something that could tangibly connect her to what had happened, assure her that it had been real, not an imagined fantasy, a dream that confuses your waking day. By Friday, despondent and inconsolable, Mina refused to go out for dinner with friends, choosing instead to hide in the squalor of her flat, with her cat and the TV for company. A sad microwave meal and a large glass of wine eased Mina into a fretful sleep, and she woke late, unrefreshed and feeling more miserable than ever. With pure, stubborn spitefulness, rather than determination, she decided to punish herself still further by forcing her body to go for a run, something she had hated, but endured for a couple of years now. Dressing haphazardly, she tied back her hair, sorted her music, and disappeared enthusiastically up the road, hoping as usual, that she wouldn't meet anyone that she knew.

Twenty minutes later, scarlet red and heaving, Mina grasped both sides of the front door frame, attempting to feign vague attempts at stretching, rather than a desire to stay upright. The world was spinning slightly, as she fumbled in her pocket for the key and an escape from the glare of the street. Opening the front door, she spotted amongst the delivered adverts and unrequested brochures, an ominous brown envelope addressed to her. She grabbed at it, still a little cautious on her shaking legs and pushed the junk mail with her foot to the side of the hallway. It felt slightly lumpy, like it contained documents of some sort, and it was hand-addressed, a mature and fluent style, perhaps done in real ink? She stood upright and took a deep breath before scaling the stairs to her flat with renewed energy.

Sitting at her kitchen table, Mina read and re-read the short note.

'Dearest Mina,

Thank you for being a wonderful wedding conspirator. What can I say...you made a potentially tedious event exceptionally memorable.

Forgive me for not phoning as I promised. I have been away on business and only returned home a couple of days ago.

Please find enclosed details for next weekend. Presumptuous I know, but well, here's hoping you'll take a deep breath and leap with me. D x

In her left hand, Mina rubbed her thumb over the enclosed itinerary, a return flight to New York, details of how to apply for an ESTA and Daniel's address. Shocked, she sat silently in her sweaty running gear, unable to think straight, unable to comprehend what had just happened. The idea that she could, that she would, drop everything and fly across the Atlantic Ocean to meet a stranger, a man she'd met for only a couple of hours, was incomprehensible. What sort of woman did he think she was? She thought back to that sweaty, childhood classroom, the carefully written poem, the look of pity and hate in her classmates' eyes. Feeling cross, she flounced into the shower and stood under the water, rubbing at her already pink skin, her mind whirling. The steam rose around her. She began to feel hot, rivulets running down the wall of the compact and windowless room. It was an absurd offer and one that she was going to refuse. She was confident of that. Perhaps send a brief 'thank you', a short, beautifully written card or a nonchalant email. The response had to reflect her character, present the right impression, create the appropriate mood for any future liaison with the very charming Daniel.

'You're not seriously thinking of going, are you?' Nicole's shocked face was smiling. 'I mean, you know nothing about him. American Psycho and all of that.' Mina started smiling too. 'He'll have you tied up, slicing off bits. Unless that's what you are hoping for?'

'Don't be ridiculous!' Though the thought had

crossed her mind once or twice.

'Why would Lucy and Simon know someone who

tortures unsuspecting girls for a living. You know I can't go. How would I get time off work? Besides, how keen would that look? Chasing him across the ocean?'

The Media café was busy, and Mina found herself automatically lowering her voice. It felt demeaning to be discussing this proposal in this environment.

'You've got a week to decide. I mean you can't send the tickets back, can you? You'll easily make the flight if you could get cover for the last two lessons of the afternoon. I could cover you. Couldn't you have some important doctor's appointment that you booked weeks ago?' Mina had thought it all through – the excuses, the logistics, the idea. Finally, she'd phoned Nicole and asked her out to lunch, desperately needing advice. 'What do we even know about him?'

'Not a lot…I think that's my point. Lucy said she'd seated me between two bachelors – so we know that they're supposedly single. Other than that, very little.'

'Well, what about at the wedding, did you learn anything then? Did you know he lived in New York?'

'Are you kidding? I didn't interrogate him. Just danced and kissed a little'. She thought back to his piercing eyes staring at her – the engorged moon lighting his soft, wavy hair and the touch of his fingertips.

'Well, he's obviously got some money. Your average guy doesn't send air tickets to a girl he briefly danced and flirted with at a party. You have mutual friends – hence the wedding invitation. Besides, he didn't batter you to death in the woods. That would have been a perfect place.'

'Nicole!'

'And you seemed pretty smitten when we spoke on that Sunday afternoon. How long did you stay with him before?'

'I didn't.'

'What do you mean?'

'I didn't. We walked…kissed a little…re-joined the party and I got my taxi home.'

'Really!' Nicole appeared genuinely surprised. 'So, you're telling me that this Daniel character, kisses you, returns home alone and then sends you the airfare. You must have made some impression!'

'Stop it. Don't you think I'm asking myself the same question? I have no idea why I would even consider it – it's ridiculous.' Their soup arrived, and the conversation paused while the waiter presented their bowls and retrieved their empty cups.

'It's pretty exciting too. Oh, come on Mina. Has anything like this ever happened before? Let's be honest'.

'Yeah, all the time. Course not…got to be honest, not that much ever happens to me.'

'So, where's the harm?'

'Do you want the list?' Images of American Psycho flashed before her, a sharp knife delicately dissecting the breast tissue of a bound and alert

33

Mina. But then those eyes, penetrating pools, green and dark with longing – those hands.' It's impossible. I couldn't possibly. I mean I wouldn't even know where to begin. Who in their right mind would get on a plane and fly transatlantic to meet a stranger? Come on – would you Nicole?'

'Well. It's a bit different for me.'

'Exactly. Why is it different for you? Because you have a boyfriend? Because you don't like flying? I need a way to bow out gracefully and I have just under a week to do it.'

7 NEW ALLIANCES

The first time he saw her he knew. He'd been sat alone at the wedding, making small talk with a group of strangers, when she'd walked in. It was her hat he noticed first, the wide black brim shadowing her face, pert red lips pouting mischievously amongst porcelain skin. Her vision limited, she was finding it hard to navigate her way through the tables and collected guests. One long-gloved hand pinched the brim. keen for it to stay solid. whilst the other felt its way through the throng. He watched her mesmerized. The chatter around him dimming, her body easing gently between chairs, her lips mouthing apologies as her hat brushed accidently against guests, every movement provocatively innocent. When she finally wriggled into the seat next to him, his heart was racing. He was only conscious of her parted rouged lips, slightly damp from the wine and her musky-sweet scent. She was quietly loud, demanding the attention of everyone on the table, though saying very little. Their knees brushed, and he found himself mumbling a regrettable apology, whilst wishing that he could run his hand across her thigh and discard it there for eternity. He watched intently as she eased off the long gloves, pulling each finger methodically, and gently clapped and smiled at the newly-weds. Once seated again, he found it difficult to engage her in conversation, she seemed intent on those sat opposite and he instead, was subjected to the minutiae of another couple's planned vows.

He knew he had to have her. It was as simple as that. When the meal was over, and she'd excused herself, he watched her elegantly work her way back through the tables and out of the reception hall, the curve and sway of her walk, the tight calves perched high, her elongated neck. He watched her return, unashamedly voyeuristic, every move, every smile, pleasuring him.

He knew she would be his, it was just a matter of time.

8 PASTURES NEW

Business class was nice. Mina had curled up in the spacious seat, a glass of bubbly in one hand and a new book discarded on her lap. Even the pre-flight lounge had been nice, quiet, and sombre, away from the throngs of travellers perched expectantly on plastic chairs. Too excited to sleep, and too worried to read, she'd watched films back-to-back the entire way. Packing had been stressful, a microcosm of her wardrobe, each piece selected and analysed for fit, look and impression. Few items had made it into the case, and she'd had a couple of manic evenings of self-loathing standing in brightly lit fitting rooms. The hat – job completed – had been royally wrapped in tissue paper, gently placed in its box and perched on top of a wardrobe, away from prying cat claws. The flight deck was quiet. Some couples away for a romantic weekend and the odd business traveler returning home. As the plane prepared for landing, Mina's heart bounced loudly, and she had a sudden urge to vomit.

In the baggage collection hall, having her

painstakingly chosen possessions in one compact case, Mina dawdled needlessly. She needed the pause, the space, the breath to muster the courage to walk outside of the arrivals hall. The world where he belonged, and she was a stranger. The world a stranger had invited her to. She joined the lengthy, winding, immigration queue which rippled noiselessly with tension; passengers silently clutching their passports and avoiding eye-contact. Mina too felt their fear. Security officers loitered intentionally, their uniforms deliberately menacing, their fingertips resting ominously on their guns. It was late, but she was alert and wary. Mina felt less like a romantic heroine in this snaking queue, more unidentified terrorist on foreign soil. The gang of armed officers barking orders grew closer and Mina realized that her time was close. She knew her hands were shaking as she handed over her passport, had her fingerprints taken and endured the scornful scrutiny of Homeland Security. Then it was over, and she was swept towards the run-down and noisy arrivals hall. People grinning and waving from every side, placards with names and welcomes, announcements, and trollies. She reached the end of the corridor and realized that she was alone, helpless, stupid, a child in a city a long way from home. She hadn't anticipated this moment but knew it definitely hadn't been this. Her heart was pounding, and she felt a wave of grief and panic sweep over her.

'Hi, Mina.' He called softly, touching the top of her shoulder,' Sorry, didn't mean to be late, freeway traffic'. She turned her head quickly – took one look at his smiling eyes and burst into uncontrollable tears.

'I don't normally get that reaction,' He smiled, pulling her close to his chest, so that her shudders could subside privately.

In the taxi, they sat quiet and apart. Mina stared out at the bright lights, embarrassed by her performance and conscious that she was already an expensive disappointment. There seemed no need for chit-chat. She sensed an early morning flight would probably be inevitable and was wondering how she could organize this. Was frantically working out the time difference so that she might ring Nicole for help.

When the taxi finally stopped forty-five minutes later, she realized they were outside a bar, not his apartment as she'd anticipated. He helped her outside into the hot, spring night and straight into the bowels of a surprisingly chilly club. It was dark and full, an orchestra of voices talking over the lone jazz pianist. Mina was thankful on both counts, hoping in the darkness, he wouldn't see her puffy, smudged eyes or try to make elaborate conversations.

'Are you hungry? They do great nachos here. Or a burger perhaps…fries?' She nodded, compliant, and allowed herself to be led to a booth in the far corner of the room. Whilst he disappeared, Mina quietly surveyed her image in the wall mirrors and reapplied some lip gloss and eye liner. He returned beaming with two bottles of beer and slid in next to her – their thighs touching. She could smell the scent from his skin.

'I'm sorry,' She began, 'It was a long flight'.

'Hey, honestly, it's fine. I'm just glad you came. Not sure you would…it was a bit of a long shot.' Mina smiled for the first time since arriving.

'Up until lunchtime, I wasn't sure whether I was coming either. Your invite was a bit of a surprise you know'.

'I know. Sorry. We just sort of left it didn't we? At the wedding I mean. You know, we just sort of parted, and I don't know, you've been on my mind, quite a lot actually. So, I thought, why not. Nothing ventured as they say. Might as well ask.' They clinked bottles and Mina took a gulp of the cold and fizzy beer, relaxing into the leather seat and the warmth of Daniel's thigh.

Their food arrived. Bountiful amounts of fries and fiery, chilli nachos. As they ate, Mina began to breathe again, and their conversation grew. He explained that he'd moved to New York the year before on business, initially for six months and that he'd stayed. He travelled the world a lot but considered this to be his current home for the time being. He knew Lucy and Simon whilst at university and though pleased for the happy couple, had been dreading the wedding.

'All those rituals and speeches, bells and smells. Just not my thing really. You were well, you know, like a breath of fresh air walking in alone, in that huge hat'.

'I was dreading it too. Not used to functions on my own.' Mina lied, quickly drinking from the bottle in case he smelled her insecurity.

'Are you tired, or do you fancy exploring?'

He paid the bill and they ascended onto the surprisingly busy sidewalk. It was hot. A sticky, contagious heat that clung to their skin, smearing it with the residue and grime of the city. They walked, casually holding hands, Mina showing due surprise and awe at every landmark he pointed out. He appeared to enjoy being her personal guide – maneuvering her down side streets, regularly hiding her eyes before revealing personal landmarks and favourite attractions. They smiled and talked, dodging the throngs of people either dawdling or pushing through. Mina relaxed, warming to the situation she had put herself in. Two complete strangers in a big city, miles away from home.

A neon sign guided them to a large and impersonal bar, where they managed to find two seats and a bottle of wine.

'You must think it strange that I came.'

'Why? I invited you. Why would it be strange that you took me up on the offer?'

'I don't know…it's just not the sort of thing I normally do.'

'It's not the sort of thing I normally do. Don't ask me why. It felt sort of right…you know, the right thing to do. I suddenly felt lonely here…for the first time. I mean I have friends, a life, a stressful job…but it felt odd somehow…sort of vacant. Does that make sense?' Mina nodded, not quite sure what he meant at all. Sensing her reticence, he added, 'Perhaps I just thought it might be fun…to see you again…to be with you.'

'I hope I'm not disappointing.' Daniel gripped her hand and looked at her.

'Absolutely not. Shall we dance?' They left her bag with a bartender that Daniel obviously knew and made their way downstairs to the dance floor. A DJ perched high above the crowd conducted the proceedings with dignity and finesse, stretching his arms wide and leading the crowd through each peak and fall. There was a sweaty excitement in the room, an anarchistic clash of drums and bodies, as strangers gyrated and twirled, thumped and pumped. Mina, the warm wine taking effect, felt her inhibitions slide as Daniel pulled and squeezed her into the throng of the crowd. Quickly she found her beat, her movements intense and sexual, Daniel's eyes on her throughout. A timid ripple of sweat sat between her breasts as she thrust and vibrated, her eyes bright, her smile wide. Orchestrated and led, the swell of bodies moved as one, liberated and oblivious, hearts beating in unison, they performed. At times, her arms raised high, Daniel clutched Mina close, smelling her hair, kissing the nape of her damp neck. But she couldn't stay still, intoxicated by the rhythm she squirmed away, turning her back, her hips uncontrolled, she coquettishly peeped over her shoulder to see Daniel's approving eyes. Breathless and consumed, they found intimate solitude in the mass, both knowing where this was going, both compliant in the plan. When eventually they stepped out onto the noisy sidewalk and hailed a cab, the unspoken culmination of heady wine and physical desire glued them together as they travelled the short distance back to Daniel's apartment.

9 THE DESIRE OF STRANGERS

Mina felt awkward. Sat nervously on the corner of his couch, she examined the broken flesh around her fingertips, dissecting at will small pieces of flesh. She was chilly, goosebumps running along the down on her arms, and she was aware of her nipples, contained and erect inside the thin fabric of her dress. One finger began to bleed, a tiny abrasion pumping a continuous and unstoppable trickle of blood. Annoyed, she stuck it into her mouth and sucked hard, conscious of the mess it might inflict on the cream couch. It was quiet, the sound of car horns and traffic muffled by the 40th floor and sound-proof glass, the soundtrack to some other world. Daniel entered with two whiskies, and she stood to meet him, combatant, the finger still protruding, small gulps of blood oozing. Silently, they swallowed hard and fast, sensing the heat rise through their throats and tingle the delicate skin of their lips. Then they collided. A tangle of urgency and force, a need to inhabit the skin of the other. They grabbed and groped each other in a fierce frenzy, bodies grinding and teeth clashing. Breathless, they paused momentarily, while Daniel unzipped the back of her dress and she let it fall to the ground. Daniel dropped to the floor in front of her, kissing the top of her lace panties, the faint line of downy hair visible, to her naval, then up higher, his hands searching ahead, squeezing and kneading, finally pinching her nipples before his full mouth came down hard on them. Mina couldn't breathe – her hands grasped and groped – begging him, pleading with him.

She didn't ask herself what she was doing and certainly didn't contemplate the consequences. It had begun and therefore had to end.

Twenty minutes later, spent and panting, they lay next to each other on the rug, naked and silent. Their fingertips silently reached for each other and entwined steadfastly, their pulses racing in unison. They stared at each other, searching, transfixed, while their chests, still gasping for air, gradually calmed. Her face tingled, blood still flushed on her cheeks, her hair splayed on the white rug. Neither dared rupture their connection with a word. Neither wanting to be wrenched back into the civilities. Below the world continued to shout, gesticulate, and rest on its horns. They continued to stare at each other, wallowing in each other's gaze.

Lying against his chest, later in bed, Mina listened to his steady, quiet breathing. His arm, slender and strong, pinned her against the sheets and she gently stroked its silky hair, careful not to wake him. Sporadically, she moved her nose noiselessly over his skin, breathing his musky scent and smell, keen to digest the moment, afraid of what the morning light might bring. She closed her eyes feeling comfort in this desired tower of captivity.

The next twenty-four hours were a whirlwind of walking, shopping, dinners, and wine bars. Mina began to believe she was on a film set, so familiar was she with the sights and sounds of the New York landscape. However, in the pit of her stomach grew the fear that she'd been given a sneak preview of this world, one she could never inhabit, before being spitefully sent back to the teenage grime and angst of her mundane job in London. Every time, she caught Daniel's eye, this thought of separation seemed impossible. However, Mina was a realist and knew that exportation home alone was inevitable. Daniel for his part, appeared to enjoy having her around. That first Saturday morning, he'd arrived bedside with fresh coffee and warm pastries and while they'd cooled, Daniel and Mina had caressed and kissed, exploring, and touching until their joint agony exploded in a ferocious and fierce climax. Spent, they then showered and wandered in the sunshine, ambling and talking, oblivious to the frenetic Manhattan Saturday shoppers tutting around them. They rode the ferry to Stratton Island, rode the subway to Central Park and drank champagne: it was a world of *Breakfast at Tiffanys*. A world Mina didn't want to leave.

On the final night, they meandered quietly, hands clasped, across Brooklyn Bridge. It was a sultry hot night. The scene lit by the backdrop of skyscrapers and the sky sprinkled haphazardly with stars whilst an orderly line of airplane lights hovered menacingly, waiting for their slot to land.

Daniel and Mina were comfortingly quiet – the odd finger point to a place of interest on the landscape – a shared smile. It felt still. The moon, pregnant and full, lit Mina's face, her eyes bright. Daniel stopped and enveloped her in his arms, his head close to her ear, his breath warm against her skin.

'It's the moon that keeps us safe in the dark, makes the tide ebb and flow, lights us home, inhabits our hearts so that they glow wise and free.' She could feel the surge of his chest against her back, the quiet breathing. He pulled her closer and she instinctively pressed her fingertips tightly into his naked arms. Around them, tourists talked excitedly, took selfies, pointed and gesticulated. Mina and Daniel stayed motionless, hung in an isolated pocket of their emotions, content and warm. Neither wanted to speak. Their silence circled them reassuringly. Their touching skin tingled with the anticipation. They were a frozen image in a frenzy of human movement.

A crack of lightening directly above them broke the suspense. Mina jumped and squeezed Daniel's arm. Within minutes, regular and ferocious, lightening cut through the blackness illuminating the bay and encouraging the bridge dwellers to hasten their steps. Large droplets of warm rain began to fall, slow at first and then quicker, dissolving on contact with hair, clothes, shoes. They began to run, eyes partially closed, weaving in and out of those already looking for shelter, squealing with equal amounts of horror and glee. At last, soaked and dripping, they saw an Irish bar, bright, steaming and inviting. A final push and they were inside, grinning at each other, bedraggled and dripping, while the owner glowered at them from behind the bar.

Later, in his apartment, showered and naked, Mina lay on the white sheets stroking the delicate hair around his nipples.

'Thank you.' She said.

'For what?'

'Everything. You know this weekend. It's been great. I.'

'Hey, don't say anything…please.' Daniel leaned on his elbow, straddling Mina with his hairy thigh, and placed two fingers delicately on her lips. 'You are so beautiful.' She felt his cock stir against her leg as his mouth came down and his tongue entered her.

10 HOME

Home felt shabby, small, and dated: a clutter of pointless items and an empty bed. Mina lay spread-eagled on the bed, hands still clasping the front door keys and the handle of her bag and stared at the opaque swirls on the ceiling. It was late, perhaps four in the morning and eerily quiet. She'd tried to sleep on the plane, though ended up watching back-to-back movies in order to focus her mind and not allow it to think. She needed to be up for work in two hours but knew that sleep was impossible. She felt vacant and miserable and terribly alone. The cat, pleased to see her, fussed around her face purring loudly, its wet nose pushed against her cheek, its fluff irritating her nose. Sighing, she hoisted her body off the bed, carried the cat to its bowl and fed her. It was chilly, and the kitchen smelt damp with a hint of cat meat and curry remnants. She looked out at the pocket yard below, the bins lined up, the high wall and glass fragments cemented to the top. Victorian London felt claustrophobic and dingy. Returning to her bedroom, she crawled under the covers and flicked the switch on the TV, cascading up and down the channels, catching glimpses, watching nothing.

Their goodbye at the airport had been quiet and timid. They'd had lunch, a brief walk in Central Park and then a cab ride to the airport. They'd dealt with practicalities. Did she want a coffee? Would she be able to get a taxi at the other end? Did she have her passport? The airport, dreary and unassuming had helped. There was no elegant concourse, no romantic rail-side café just passport control and security; it was obviously easier to get out, than get in. They'd stalled slightly at security, hovering, a moment of hesitation in which they'd smiled at each other, the unspoken spoken. Finally, she'd bravely reached up, kissed him carefully on the lips, turned her back and was gone. She didn't allow herself to turn back, for fear of…she couldn't contemplate that. Instead, she'd focused on her bags and her passport – feeling his eyes boring into the back of her head as he stood motionless in the crowd watching and waiting. Her eyes felt strange and she had to blink several times to stop them watering, then she was alone in the departure lounge, every couple reminding her of her own lonely journey home.

The alarm screamed, and Mina woke abruptly, conscious of a pain in her neck, the TV on and her coat collar rubbing her chin. She licked her dry lips, felt the heavy makeup caked on her skin, slid out of bed and showered. It was only afterwards that she realized she'd shed his smell, his muskiness. She had inadvertently scrubbed and washed him away. No identifiable sense of him being in her world at all. A mirage merely, a thought, some lonely woman's sad dream.

Cleansed completely of her weekend, she dressed, scraping back her hair and cradled a hot coffee while she caught ten minutes of the news. This was it then. They hadn't arranged another meeting. Hadn't sworn their affinity. Hadn't made promises they had no intention of keeping. They'd had a weekend. A glorious, wonderful, exuberant weekend of flesh and lips and fingers and…Mina, agitated, grabbed for her jacket and slammed the front door behind her.

The staffroom smelt and looked like a hospital waiting room. Lines of padded chairs meticulously placed. Some back-to-back like an elaborate game of musical chairs, some taken and protected, a pile of exercise books indicating the owner. Coffee cups, school dinner plates and half eaten packets of biscuits decorating the floor slovenly. Mina felt Nicole's arm on her shoulder as she stood in front of the pigeonholes.

'Well? You look suitably tired. He didn't murder you then?' Mina smiled wanly. 'Are you going to see him again?'

'Hard to say really.' She didn't hide the disappointment.

'Was it that bad? Seriously? He must have wined and dined you. Was he weird, you know, expecting all sorts?' Mina thought back to their Sunday morning of elaborate exploration. The buzzer blasted, and both flinched. 'No one said anything about you phoning in sick yesterday. Not a word. Cover supervisors to the rescue. Catch you later?' Mina nodded in agreement, and both filed out onto the busy corridor and were subsumed amongst the pulsating throng of blazers, hairdos and hormones.

The first month passed insufferably slowly in a frenzy of lesson planning, marking, teenage confrontations and loneliness. As the days passed and Mina heard nothing, the void in her chest grew. She'd sent a brief and cautiously chosen text, to thank him for his hospitality and attempt to put into words the connection she thought they had. This 'connection' was in fact a surge of painful and indiscriminate feelings. Her pores were alive and pulsating. Her every thought was of him, his lips, his eyes, the touch of his chest, the tips of his fingers, his cock, his taste...she was consumed with desire, great swathing surges rising in her chest, painful and all encompassing. She hurt her way through each day, feeling solitude acutely for the first time. At times, she found herself gazing at a wall, subsumed with feeling, a touch, a look, those eyes. Brought back to earth by a repeated 'miss' fired indiscriminately in her direction. She began to build her protective shell, inch by inch, hour by hour. She couldn't allow herself to be vulnerable, had been there several times before, knew the intolerable pain and humiliation. So, her text had been precise, appropriate and on reflection, quite cool. In response, she'd heard nothing and as the minutes ticked into hours, ticked into days, ticked into weeks, Mina began to actively reinforce her protective outer shell. She was bad tempered in class, snapped at colleagues and non-committal with friend's invites. Those around her assumed the weekend had gone badly and many were loath to broach the subject. Instead, they kept their conversations brief, focused on work and whenever possible, they avoided her. This suited Mina, boarded up in her own misery, she volunteered for extra duties and escaped to the sanctuary of her own flat as much as possible.

When Daniel finally replied, it was by post, not text. A letter, long and detailed, describing his emotions and thoughts following their 'exquisite' time together and apologizing profusely for his elusive behaviour. Mina tingled as she read it, but the void in her stomach had already begun to calcify and her newly acquired cynicism began to highlight the absurdity of this long-distance, romantic entanglement. She didn't write back.

11 FESTIVAL FEVER

Another month passed, and the sulky summer weather dampened Mina's spirits still further. She woke to the rain, went to work in the rain, did break duty in the rain and waited for her train home in the rain. Damp and desolate, the dank greyness of London permeated the four walls of her compact flat making it increasingly confined. Her only respite was the glimmer of excitement presented by her annual pilgrimage to the festival. This was her weekend of glory, her moment of freedom and folly, tinged with a sprinkling of insanity, away from the regimented conformity of school life. It was an opportunity to indulge in a make-believe world of fairy dust, dressing up, music, sex and mud. Living conditions more extreme than a refugee camp didn't dissuade Mina and her three friends from consuming three heady days of debauchery neatly wrapped up and presented as a music festival. They planned their outfits in advance, helped Nicole clean and decorate her camper van and hunted down boxes of tasteless wine to keep them hydrated. Mina, still carrying

Daniel like a shadow, began to view this year's festival as catharsis, a way of purging Daniel's touch, a way of liberating her from the overwhelming and unrealistic sense that she was missing him. Therefore, early one Thursday afternoon, the girls discarded their work clothes, donned wellies and fluorescent pink angel wings and began their long journey to nirvana.

Mina grinned uncontrollably as she stood on the hill looking out at the huge, effervescent city below. A million lights twinkled, interspersed with illuminated domes emitting an array of sounds, all consolidated by the unifying boom of the bass, rhythmic and in perfect time with her heartbeat. For the first time in months, she felt a sense of potential liberation. The temporary city below, 100 square miles of eccentric extravagance and hedonistic happiness, emitted warmth and possibility. It was dark, damp and completely electrifying. Campervan parked up, beds made and essentials in hand, they began their long, slippery descent to the demonic paradise below. The layered, corrugated iron security fences added to their excitement as they waited in line to be searched, tagged and admitted. Walking was difficult, each booted step precise and deliberate, as they slurped each foot in and then out, moon-walking forwards, eyes set firmly on the prize ahead. The two hundred thousand inhabitants of this imaginary real world were sucked sanctimoniously into the earth; mud and fluids colliding, locked firmly down so that they couldn't flutter and fly skywards like their wings suggested. The girls ploughed on, smiles bright and sincere, minds focused on the plan, a couple of bands, then Shangri-La until morning. Mina felt her heart warm again, the outer hard circle of her protective shield began to thin ever so slightly. She realized it was all still working. She was smiling, her blood was still flowing hard and full, her heart wasn't broken. Surrounded by people, the comfort of strangers, sharing their sweat and smells, she immersed herself, pushing on into the throng, determined to explore and play.

They came suddenly out of the darkness. A collection of clowns, diverse in size and character, walking in slow motion through the crowds, a corrupt and sinister version of the opening of Tarantino's Reservoir Dogs, innocent to the stares as the crowds parted in their wake. Smoke, real not created, wafted around them as they walked through the teaming café area, consumed by falafels, curries and pies. Mina, ever so slightly tipsy, watched the clowns with her mouth gaping, not able to digest the image, nervous and enthralled; excited. As a child, clowns had scared her, caused many a fitful night of terrors and anxiety. Now, pushing the half-eaten supper aside, Mina stood silently and watched them as they strolled confidently past. Then raising her arms high, she yelled at Daniel's shadow.

'Fuck you! I don't want you – leave me alone...fuck off.' She wasn't convinced, but she thought she saw the final clown in the pack look back and wink. Then they were absorbed into the crowd, anonymous and fictional. The girls, clad in pink feathers and leather, began their trek, attracting exactly the wrong sort of desired attention from stockbrokers dressed as grannies and the cast of YMCA flaunting their pecks. It was a Mad Max's Midsummer Night's Dream of voyeurism and hedonistic fetish. Mina forgot the exercise books, her dingy flat and the cat. Instead, she was Titania on coke, absorbed in her displayed skin, her pert buttocks and breasts adorned with nipple studs and glitter. Mina was attracting attention and it felt good. She watched the performances, her body twitching and pulsing. She throbbed and vibrated. She threw her long hair left to right, alive and flighty, her feet sucked and bound into the rich earth. Around her were the beautiful people, the lovers of life, the unafraid. They beat and shuddered, caught in the rhapsody of the rhythm, grins entrenched on their faces, eyes euphoric. The real world seemed separate and alien, something not to contemplate. Nicole, brave and beautiful, rode the shoulders of a stranger, waving her arms skyward – her breasts naked - nipples erect – oozing sex and inspiring jealousy and admiration. Mina allowed herself to move in time with the crowd, waves of movement, sometimes fluid, sometimes wet with beer and aggression. She danced ritualistically, shuddering and grinding, her eyes closed, oblivious to those around her. She had no idea of time, just knew she had to continue. Each pulsating bass moving her hips forward and back. The performing flame throwers igniting, not extinguishing, her need to live, to feel, to love. She danced like her life depended on it, tribal and instinctive, gripped by the freedom the setting and her body allowed.

In the early hours, finally spent, Mina and her three friends sat silently on a wooden bench, mugs of coffee in hand, breasts on display, wings in place. The glitter on their faces awry, the lip-gloss long gone and splatters of mud decorating each thigh, they were still laughing, still smiling, still available. Mina reached across to dip a fat, greasy chip in the curry sauce. She felt slightly dizzy and wasn't sure she'd make the long climb back up the hill to the camper van. Music throbbed around them and her toes were feeling cold and tingly inside the confines of her boots.

'Hi. It's Mina, isn't it? Lucy's wedding...we were sat next to each other. Remember? I'm Alec.' Mina's head looked up at the smiling face, the white teeth shining in his dark face. 'Do I need fairy dust to enter?' Mina was briefly confused then remembered her attire, remembered it enough to move a hand across her tassel-covered nipples.

'Sorry. I...it's been a long night...yes, Mina. Nice to meet you. Again.' She stretched out a hand, sinking slightly lower on the bench to hide her protruding breasts that were suddenly feeling very naked. Alec sank very low in an exuberant and theatrical bow. 'May we join you?' Mina looked at her friends who shrugged agreement. 'Let me introduce you...Harry, Raj and Samps.' Mina returned the compliment, introducing her fairies as one might delegates at a political conference. There was no formal request for coupling, the six merely merged into a group. There was much ruffling of feathers, fingers accidently brushing flesh and nipples, hilarity and laughter. They moved to the

Rum-Shack, an area housing a teething mass of bodies moving in unison, a congregation responding dutifully to the DJ minister at the front, as they chanted the words 'rum shack' repeatedly. Next a retro tent, drinking vodka shots, dancing to 90s tracks and chasing inflatable balloons and bubbles. Mina and her friends, fought for the podiums, grinded and wriggled, exhibited and performed. As the moon started to retreat, began its slow, cautionary descent, Alec and Mina slowly navigated the endless fields of mud.

When dawn finally broke, the desolation of the temporary refugee camp became apparent. The festival goers, humans by nature, wired to survive and desperate to mark their territory, had created an array of dwellings to protect them from the rain and suggest their affinities. Gazebos and ground sheets strewn between tents – flags marking territory, highlighting respective tribes, football teams or life choices. Some 'camps' were organized; tables, chairs, a candle chandelier hanging precariously from a sturdy pole. Some resembled the post-apocalyptic world, the fabric of the tent submissively crushed into the mud, crumpled, wet, forlorn, and hopefully vacant. Alec's abode, purposely pitched on a well-drained plot had a sense of order and cleanliness around the tiny encampment of 4 tents, sat amidst the surrounding chaos. A central gazebo lit with a hundred twinkling lights and decorated with hanging wind chimes. Reaching into his tent, Alec produced two plastic beakers, a Ribena bottle full of wine and a thick, wool blanket, which he wrapped gently around

Mina's shoulders to keep her warm. Gratefully she accepted his help to remove wellies, thick with cloying mud and dripping wings and to put on a fresh pair of fluffy dry socks. Sitting next to him on the inflatable sofa, cross-legged, squaw-like under the blanket, pink feathers still in her hair, Mina closed her eyes and drank the surprisingly good wine. Though nearly four-thirty, the chaotic, pulsating world around them continued, oblivious to the time. A consistent stream of revellers trudged slowly passed them, rain hoods up – laughter – voices. Music pounded from all sides, a diverse and complimentary mix of drums and rhythms. Mina felt sheltered and quiet. Alec talked, his voice deep and guttural, about his love of music, his guitar, his joy at seeing her. Mina listened, her fragile hands protruding out of the blanket to grasp the beaker he continued to fill. Now and again, she allowed herself to peek at his animated face under the gasoline lamp and sparkling lights. She was conscious of her glittered nakedness under the blanket, the somewhat itchy tutu and sequins pinching delicate flesh. Without warning, he leant across and kissed her full on the mouth, his warm tongue exploring, the fruity taste of warm wine. He caressed her neck and wet hair, allowing his kisses to explore her face, eyelids, icy hands. Finally, he eased her from the inflatable sofa and gently pulled her into the confines of his tent, zipping the world out and laying her on the rugs and blankets strewn throughout. He unpeeled her blanket, his fingertips traversing the length of her body in long, gentle strokes, up and down. She removed her tassels, allowing her breasts to breathe, their dark nipples erect and welcoming as he sucked and kneaded them. Inches above them the rain loudly pelted the roof and they could hear voices laughing, talking. Inside, they were silent and intent. Mina, cocooned in this nomadic enclave, stretched as he played, her vagina wet and ready. When finally he turned her onto her stomach and removed her panties, both knew that it would be quick and urgent.

Spent, they pulled the blanket over their conjoined bodies and fell into a deep slumber. Outside, the party continued, loud and intense. Inside, the tent, womb-like, protected their safe solitude.

What woke them was the silence, the absence of sound or motion, just a faint trickle of rain running off the sides of the tent. They were warm, their naked bodies still connected. Alec pressed his head into the small of her neck, ruffling her still damp hair and smelling her skin. Neither spoke, just lay together listening for a sound, a reason to rise, an instruction that didn't come. An hour passed in which he stroked her hair and they kissed aimlessly, bodies teasing each other, both nervous to lose the covers for fear of the fresh morning air. Finally, Mina seated herself upon him, looking down at his dark chest and rode him silently and deliberately, masking his moans with her hand, enjoying the performance and the rise and fall of her naked breasts.

Gradually, the world cautiously began to rise. Mina, wriggled into some borrowed clothes, ran her hands through her hair and climbed feet-first out of the tent. Outside, Alec smiled at her as he squatted in front of a burner, frying bacon.

'Coffee?'

'Please.' She resumed her position on the inflatable couch, mug clutched to her chest, enjoying the warmth of the hot drink. She was conscious of the crusted mud on her legs and caked glitter on her cheek bones. Alec's open smile and attentiveness revealed no criticism of the mess she clearly was.

'Here you go.' Passing her the bacon roll, Mina suddenly remembered how hungry and grateful she was. They ate silently, neither knowing how to start the conversation. A quiet snore reverberated from the neighbouring tent and a couple of times they looked at each other and giggled. She stretched her legs across his lap and he rubbed her socked feet.

'I must go soon. They'll wonder where I am. Might be worried.'

'Of course. Perhaps we could...you know...meet later?'

'Yeh...great. That would be nice. I mean I need to check the other's plans...but yeh. Would you mind if I borrowed this t-shirt? We are a nocturnal species you see, glitter doesn't do well on a damp English morning.' Alec smiled.

'Cider bus – midnight. I can be there.' Mina once again encased in her mud boots, began the long trek back to her friends, desperate for toothpaste and knowing there would be a protracted inquisition.

By midnight, Mina surprised herself by being excited to see him. She'd spent the morning wrapped in a duvet in the van, drinking copious amounts of tea and dunking biscuits, while a make-shift line dried their wings and tutus. By three o'clock, all four girls were dressed and ready, more 'Mad Max' than 'Titania and her fairies': leather shorts, corsets, and wellies. By six o'clock, the sun strained delicately through the clouds, showering streams of light across the waiting crowds to thunderous applause. The girls, faces tilted skywards, felt the renewed warmth of the early summer sunshine, and knew it was going to be a good night. At first, Mina couldn't see him, eyes analysing the throngs of people queuing at the bar. Then she saw his wave through the crowd and the girls began to squeeze and squirm their way through the maze of people, hands held tight for fear of losing each other.

'I wasn't sure you'd come'

'I had to return your t-shirt, which I've left in the van I'm afraid. Sorry.'

'No worries. Anytime.'

They talked as they joined the endless stream of people swarming to the next act, the next event, the next show. Movement was still slow due to the sodden ground and Mina was aware of cloying mud on her calves and thighs. But she glowed every time he looked at her, felt at ease in his easy banter and found herself giggling like a younger self. They all stayed together throughout the night – moving endlessly between different delights – trapeze - fire – drum and bass – dancing – food and wine. Finally, they traipsed back up the long hill to the campervans and sat around the girls' camping stove, under a starry sky and drank whiskey. Their talk was general and light and while the world below continued on its epic party, the new - found friends laughed and teased each other. As the sky began to lose its darkness and assume a mottled grey colour, the boys reluctantly said their farewells and began the walk back to their tents on the other side of the hundred-acre site. Mina watched him go, missing him immediately.

12 WANTING

He could still taste her. His clothes still impregnated with her smell...her scent...her touch. He stretched cat like across the top of his bed, smiling smugly. What a weekend. She was beautiful and bright, sensitive, and funny. He sat up and rummaged in his coat pocket, finding the crumpled paper that she'd hastily scribbled on. Picking up the phone, he dialled then stopped. What could he say? Thanks? Thanks for a great weekend? It didn't seem appropriate in the circumstances. Far too mundane and mediocre. He felt on fire, bursting, wanting to shower her with declarations. He replaced the handset and sat quietly. He needed to be careful. Couldn't let her think that he was weak, needy. What if it had just been a bit of fun, an excursion, a break from the everyday. Perhaps she was already regretting it, debasing it by describing every movement, every thrust, every kiss with her friends over coffee? Perhaps it was better left for a while. Give him time to think. Give him time to plan his response. Give him time to regroup and organize his emotions. He took a deep breath and stood, confident in his decision, his crisp, ironed shirt confirming the caution needed in these circumstances. He drank some coffee and grabbed the car keys, lingering unnecessarily by the jumper strewn over the chair back, still smelling of Mina.

13 POST-FESTIVAL FEELINGS

Post festival was always a miserable time. Tired from a long drive home and three hours sleep, Mina woke to the dread of Year 8 and the prospect of a stifling and sweaty ride on the tube. It didn't help that she'd done no preparation over the weekend and that at various points during the day she had to excuse herself to throw up in the staff toilets. It was common knowledge where they'd been and neither girl wanted to risk facing their line managers over inappropriate behaviour. Instead, they laboured through each long minute of the day, commiserating with each other's predicament at lunchtime, before crawling through an afternoon of confrontation and tedium. Finally free, both Mina and Nicole, braved the tube ride home together and she collapsed through the sanctuary of her front door.

By the following weekend, Mina decided that she really should sort the bin liner of clothes she'd brought back from the festival. The wellies had been binned on site, as Nicole had made it clear,

'Aint no mud wellies coming back in my van'. The clothes, having fermented in their damp darkness for a week, smelt earthy and putrid. Mina, rubber gloved, cautiously lifted each piece deciding to prewash in the bath before assaulting her old and slightly dodgy washing machine. When she saw the t-shirt, she instantaneously smiled, her eyes lit and a warm sensation glowed below. They hadn't arranged a follow-up, left it tantalizingly open and relaxed. Mina dropped the t-shirt into the sludge-coloured bathtub and decided to send him a chirpy and brief text message.

'I hear you have something that belongs to me?' He said as he greeted her at the door of the restaurant. Surreptitiously, she passed him the paper bag and he smiled. 'Thanks for the text. It's good to see you. You look beautiful and you're in clothes. I mean normal clothes!'

'It took me a while to decide. I have quite a collection of sequins and glitter you know.' She regretted the glib comment immediately. He looked different, mature, nice, indifferent to her comment.

'Real life is quite a shock, isn't it? It feels like that was the real world and this is merely a shadow of what it should be.'

'I know, I watch the reruns obsessively. It's never the same watching it on TV, they only focus on certain bits, the 'big' moments. They miss the quirky and the amazing.' Mina noticed he was sat quietly watching her. 'Sorry, it's a bad habit. I ramble. Please tell me to be quiet.'

'Carry on. I like it. I like watching you. I like listening to you.'

By the time he dropped her home, she had talked incessantly. They had shared stories of the weekend and back filled the parts of their pre-meeting life. Mina, happy and relaxed, talked about her job, her friendships and her aspirations. When the subject turned to the wedding however, she was diligent about omitting her walk in the woods with a stranger and the subsequent weekend. Alec, Mina realized, was witty and bright; perceptive, knowledgeable, and interesting. The boy she'd played with amongst the nomadic rugs, was in fact, an assured, confident and very cosmopolitan businessman, keen to indulge her romantic spirit and spoil her.

Within weeks, they were inseparable, a flurry of dinner parties, summer picnics and theatre trips. Mina barely had time to teach. Each monotonous day led to an evening of pleasure – of talking – of laughter – of kisses and caresses. The weeks passed in a whirl with Mina spending less and less time at her flat, the cat the only tangible reminder that she still paid the rent. Alec indulged her without guilt. He expected her on time, dressed sensuously and prepared for anything he might surprise her with. Mina began to appreciate the conflict between holding down a teaching role and inhabiting the world frequented by Alec. By the end of the summer term, having received two warnings for inappropriate conduct, lateness and the like, Mina scribbled a letter of resignation, presented it ceremoniously to the headteacher's PA and with merely her handbag, hip-walked cockily through the security gates on the last day of term and snugly into the leather confines of Alec's waiting car.

14 THE SUMMER OF LOVE

Alec's island house was small and intimate, three small rooms with a long and sheltered veranda overlooking a tiny and tranquil bay. Stone built it was cool inside, protecting the inhabitants from the scorching August sun. The tiled veranda was littered with a selection of loungers and a particularly elaborate baroque chaise-longue. Mina could see where Alec's rug fetish had grown; the house was adorned with an array of handmade eiderdowns over fresh, white sheets and richly coloured rugs and throws. Draped over a sunbed, the cool, afternoon sea breeze climbing up and across her prone body, Mina listened quietly to the inevitable and regular ripple of water on the pebbles below. The last few weeks had been a blur: early morning swims, blistering mornings and cool afternoon naps in the welcome breeze, the evenings sprinkled with simple dinners in homely tavernas drinking local wine. Alec, often on the phone or online to colleagues about work, left Mina to the luxury of reading romantic Victorian novels or sleeping in the sunshine. Mina, engrossed in this new world, gave little thought to the world she had forsaken other than the odd scrap of meat given to a local stray as recompense for leaving her own cat at home.   One evening, having been invited to a festival in the local village, they sat close together on plastic chairs, drinking home-made spirits, supplied by the major and surveyed the scene. Large, extended families shared tables of food, some getting up to dance or shout loudly at others. Young women, sat in the protection of their fathers and brothers, found reasons to excuse themselves and wandered languorously between the tables, brushing coyly against the bodies of waiting young men.   Alec held her hand tight.   The moon, swollen and bright, allowed them to breathe again, away from the spiteful rays of the sun.   They felt quiet and peaceful, an oasis amongst the frivolous bedlam of the festivities.

'I may have to go back to England for a few days next week. Something's come up in work and I can't really deal with it here.'

'That's fine. When?'

'Monday.   You can stay here. I won't be gone long. You may as well enjoy the sunshine for a bit longer.'

'I'll come with you. It's fine.'

'No really Mina. I want you to stay. I'll only be gone a couple of days. You won't even notice that I'm gone.'   She smiled and touched his face.

'Don't be daft. Beginning to wonder what I'd do without you.'

'Come on, let's have a go at this dancing lark', and he pulled her to her feet, grabbing the back of her cotton frock and spinning her in and out of the other couples, heads thrown back, laughing.

It was true. In the evenings, she sat alone on the veranda, staring out over the bay at the passing ships, imagining their cargo, the shadows glimpsed on deck, their stories, lives. Mina filled her days alone, exploring the island by car and by foot. She drove along dirt tracks to abandoned villages, where she walked, breathed, and marvelled, at the decaying houses and untended plots of olive groves and lemons. She sped through loud resorts, repulsed by the burger joints, tourist shops and gangs of infantile boys sunburnt and crudely tattooed. She sat reading alone on distanced pebbled beaches, comforted by her Victorian heroines and the sound of the quiet, methodical waves. Her brief and enforced solitude left her feeling still and calm. She slept soundly, the gentle waves lulling her into deep and gratifying sleep. She thought about her time with Alec, their still embryonic romance, their physical nights under the ceiling fan. She still knew so little about him. He was candid about his business, lots of conversations and emailing, little explanation. She'd never met his family and their only mutual friends were Lucy and Simon, who neither had seen since the wedding. Yet somehow the detail didn't seem to matter, didn't seem to be a priority. Even Mina's resignation wasn't causing her any current concern. She would receive her last salary on 31st August and then, well then, she hadn't given it much thought.

One blistering afternoon, the breeze not yet erect, Mina lay prostrate on the chaise longue, drifting in and out of a heat induced stupor. Lucy's words whispered menacingly, a repetitive mantra, 'one is wealthy…one is a cad…my gift to you'. Mina groaned and stretched. She didn't want to contemplate plan B, had forgotten all about her desperation and the hat, discarded and alone. This was real life, flesh and bones, fluids and heartbeats, laughter and union. She didn't want to sully her new world with that of practicalities, of bills and tubes and rain and mediocrity.

When Alec returned, she was more attentive than ever and his smile at the arrivals' gate assured her that this world was here to last. As the August sun began to fade and they prepared to return to England, Mina's only thought was of the pleasure this man brought to her life and her growing affection for him. The shadow of Daniel had dimmed, a brief moment in time, a mystical event, one she felt no need to discuss or share with anyone, let alone Alec. As he gripped her hand ready for landing, she leaned over and whispered, 'I think I love you.'

15 AN AUTUMN BREEZE

Hand-written letters are rare in the modern world – old-fashioned – somewhat quirky. You imagine them as museum pieces, elaborate, faded handwriting spilling out guttural and heart-rending emotions during times of conflict or barbarity. Lovers parted through apartheid, aggression, or war. Mothers writing to lost sons; husbands writing to wives. Their prose poetic and detailed, their feelings raw and unashamed. They took time to write and even longer to arrive, sometimes weeks, months, years. They were works of art to be treasured in metal boxes and stored, stroked and reread, the writer's cologne still permeating the parchment years after completion. Mina's letters were no different. She'd arrived home after her summer of love to find half a dozen letters hidden amongst the bills and junk mail. The neighbour, who had kept the cat alive during her absence, had reverently stacked each new day's post one on top of the other, creating a pile of envelopes and shiny adverts. Mina, dismayed by the stale smell of her flat, the tepid temperature and drizzle, left the pile untouched for several days while she attempted to freshen the flat, the cat and herself. When finally, a few days later she focused reluctantly on the pile of presumed bills, she was shocked to find six, vaguely familiar, handwritten, embossed envelopes. Resisting the urge to tear them open – she placed them to one side and forced herself to rifle through the rest, discarding the majority, those advertising bedding plants and low-cost food and mentally filing the few semi-threatening bills. When the doorbell rang, and Alec arrived to collect her for dinner, the letters remained abandoned and unopened on the side.

She returned alone the following morning, scooped up the pile of letters and sat cross-legged on the sofa, the cat nudging her expectantly, purring loudly. She didn't open them for a long while, just sat looking at the texture of the paper, the stamps, foreign and different, the familiar and flamboyant script. She felt a tinge of excitement ignite within, the shadow gradually gaining shape, the bridge, the lightening, the rain.

An hour later, the letters lay open in her lap. Mina sat back in the chair with a sigh. They were from Daniel. She didn't know what to think, her head felt muggy, and she felt nauseous. Should she feel flattered? Annoyed? Excited? Outpourings of grief and affection, detailed accounts of his travels and solitude without her. Intimate descriptions of their time together in New York. She'd assumed that out of the two, he was the wealthy one, the airfare out of the blue, the apartment. But now she began to think that she was wrong. His letters suggested some sort of correspondent, flown in to places where a news story might break, little control over his destiny or that of those close to him. They'd arrived sporadically throughout the summer, the New York address always given for the reply; a reply, however stark, that she'd failed to send. How could she? She didn't know they existed. She heard the letter box open and jumped. Her heart pounded uncontrollably. For some inexplicable reason she suddenly had the urge to find another on the mat and was thoroughly disappointed when there wasn't. Carefully, she sorted the letters into date order, reread them and then placed them back in their envelopes. Without knowing why, she found a plain paper envelope and slipped them inside, folding it over and hiding it under the hat box sat on top of her wardrobe. She felt ashamed and yet slightly warm, a little glow somewhere unseen, a betrayal not in her control.

It was several weeks before Daniel's next letter came. Mina and Alec continued as before, a couple, an item, friends. For all Alec's generosity financially, Mina was becoming a little concerned. She spent much of her week in Alec's apartment, snacking from his fridge and being treated to dinner most evenings. The September evenings were drawing in and the lonely days spent in the flat while the rest of the world worked, seemed endless. Nicole visited when she could, bringing tales from the staffroom and classroom. Mina was missed she said, the students wanted her back. But Mina knew that the chances of her returning to her job were slim. Besides, she didn't have the mental or physical energy to return. She'd purged herself of stress over the summer months and had no intention of returning to that life. Occasionally, a reminder of her predicament arrived in the form of a statement or a declined card at the cashpoint, but stoical in her resolve, she simply buried the offending letter in the settee. Occasionally, she would slip her hand under the hat box to feel the reality of the hidden envelope. However, she resisted re-reading them, resisted the urge to want something else, someone else.

When the letter arrived, Mina was apprehensive. She let it sit on the kitchen table and created chores to do before finally allowing her fingers to slide open the envelope. It was briefer this time, distinctively succinct, very different to the others, a tone of reluctant disappointment.

Dearest Mina,

I hope you are well and that life in the Metropolis is still fulfilling. I will be in London during the first week of October for work. It would be wonderful if you and I could meet, however briefly. I will be in the foyer of the Tate Modern next Friday at 10am. I fully understand if this isn't possible.

Best wishes. Daniel. X

Mina read and reread the letter. He was here in London, in the flesh, no longer a travelling shadow. The notion of a meeting was completely impossible. There was no way she was going to risk all that she had with Alec over this madness. A few sentimental letters and she would risk everything? It was a ridiculous idea.

Nicole agreed too.

'Girl, you've got to stop this haphazard style of living. Get real. You've got a great guy who loves you.'

'Well, he's never actually said that.'

'You've got a great guy who loves you.' Nicole repeated. 'Who wines and dines you all over the place. Let's be honest, life with him isn't exactly slumming it. You fancy swapping all that for a couple of dates? You'd last five minutes with my Sampson. Mina, Alec's cute, he's sensitive – you do nice things together, he's got money.'

'And I haven't?'

'Well let's face it – you don't exactly have a job at the moment, do you?'

'Let me remind you that was through choice.'

'I know, but choice doesn't pay the bills. Why screw everything up by messing with some guy you spent a couple of days with last year?'

'I dunno. I don't...I mean it. I just have this narcissistic way of destroying the good things that happen to me.'

'What's your mum say?'

'As if I'd confide in her?'

'Does she know about the job?' Mina squirmed. 'Mina?'

'I know. I just haven't got round to it. See what I mean? It's not that simple. She doesn't cope too well with disappointment, and I seem to personify it for her.'

'What's the benefit of meeting him?' Mina

picked at a piece of wool that had frayed from her jumper sleeve and sighed.

'Honestly? I don't know. It just feels like I sort of owe him. You know?'

'Not gonna lie. Not really!'

'Well, he gives me this great weekend in New York. We have a great time, then I return, he doesn't write, when he does, I act like a tantrum princess and refuse to write back. It's not exactly gratitude, is it?'

'What have you got to be grateful for? He invited you, you accepted, you spent the weekend together – come on!'

'Look, I know what you're saying. I think Alec's the one. I really do. The whole hearts and flowers thing. I just need to be sure. I've spent so long alone and now…well, two buses and all of that. What if I get on the wrong one and it goes to a dead end or worse, the bus terminal? While the other trundles off into the sunset?'

'I just don't want to see you hurt girl, that's all. You think too deeply – too intense all the time. Why not just go and see? No harm. You're allowed friends, even blokes.'

'I know – it's just.'

'Just what?' Both looked at each other, aware of what the other was thinking.

'You're right. Meeting him. Utter madness.'

16 AN OCTOBER MADNESS

By nine-thirty, Mina was sat on a shiny laminated bench, feeling decidedly sick and already regretting the decision. In front of her, the Millennium Bridge veered its way to the industrial skyline of the Tate Modern, tentatively linking both sides of the river. She'd let Alec down the night before, telling him she wasn't well, which she wasn't, so that she could focus on the decision needing to be made. Now decided, her regret was enormous. She looked up at the dome behind her and the tiny figures at the top looking out over the skyline. Was Alec there watching, binoculars in hand, ensuring her fidelity, making notes on her virtue? She moved to a less prominent bench, slightly more covert and sheltered. Pigeons pecked productively at discarded wrappers. Perhaps he worked in one of these offices? She was in central London, perhaps he was stood there now, coffee in one hand, phone in the other, looking directly at her, wondering why Mina was cowering alone on a bench outside his office. She checked her phone, no messages, no reminders. She watched workers' quickened steps, their coffees and paper bags full of sushi, quinoa and salads. A gaggle of Chinese tourists blocked her view of the bridge, excitedly arranging themselves in various poses, selfie sticks poised, and smiles rehearsed.

Reluctantly she walked towards the bridge, slowly at first, then quickening her step, keen to be amongst the swarm of people, to sustain the pace, to fulfil her decision. The smell of sweet, roasted chestnuts made her nausea more pronounced, and she felt a profound desire to pee. How did he even know she'd be available on a Friday morning? Didn't he know that she worked or at least did work full time? Had he been spying on her, collating snippets of information, after all, he appeared to be a correspondent, didn't he? Annoyed by the meandering tourists, Mina tutted her way through the crowd. Her steps continued to gather pace as she shimmered around and through groups, catching elbows as she went. She tried to control her breathing as she stepped though the enormous glass doors into the warm belly of the Tate.

The cavernous central hall was full, teaming with toddlers running at full speed up and down the enormous ramp, relishing the sound of their loud roars as they echoed and ricocheted off the high, industrial ceiling. Mina felt hot and dishevelled. Her lips felt dry, and she dug into her bag for a salve, her hands coercing the hair back into its low ponytail. The main atrium swarmed with people, moving and moving in a monotonous rhythm. She took an escalator and stood on one of the balconies – in a vantage position, searching through the crowd for any sign of the elusive Daniel. Her eyes darted, watching for any sign of familiarity, any clue or resemblance. The noise, the scale of the task and the whole surreptitious nature of this meeting, added to her growing sense of stress.

By 10.15, she was resolved to leave. She felt ridiculous and relieved, a sense of finality and resolve to the whole shortened affair. She gave the atrium one last sweep, then she turned to leave.

'Hello Mina.' Stood behind her was Daniel, his soft, wavy locks slightly hiding his playful eyes. 'Sorry, I didn't mean to startle you. I got here early and thought I'd watch for you from the top balcony.' He smiled, his eyes smiling, his lips wide over his bright smile. 'Wasn't sure you'd come, didn't think you would.' Mina was speechless, not sure what to say, an eternity between them in those ten yards. She was conscious of her eyes searching his, her body completely still, head frozen in the moment. 'Then I recognized your hair, its colour and length, thought I'd watch you for a bit. Christ that sounds creepy, doesn't it? Really creepy. Sorry.' He laughed. Mina too, though she felt a warm swell run down her spine and faint tears welled in her eyes.

'You look... well.' She said – not quite sure what to say – not quite sure why she felt such a surge of electric excitement running through her entire body – not sure why her mouth had become sterile and paralysed.

'You look amazing.'

They continued to stand, looking at each other, neither willing to make the first physical move, neither wanting to touch. She looked at his hands, remembered them softly stroking the back of her neck. Was transfixed by his lower lip, how he nervously moistened it with his tongue, that tongue.

'Shall we go somewhere, to talk? Or do you want to wander the galleries for a bit?'

Mina, still unable to utter anything meaningful, shrugged and they started to walk – in and out of the galleries, looking but not seeing, talking but not listening. He talked of his travels, his work, his life in New York. She talked of the cat, of her time relaxing alone in the sun.

'I hope I didn't embarrass you with the letters. Being away gives you time to think, to breathe. Sometimes, when I'm covering something horrific, a child's hand discarded in the road, a burnt body, I'm seeing it but not processing it. The photographer films it and I report on it. We observe atrocities and report factually. Life is real and raw like that – guttural, ephemeral. The pointless tedium of our materialistic western world seems shoddy and artificial in contrast. In that landscape the mind is forced to prioritize – on the details - on the minutiae, otherwise you don't survive. The further I flew, the more I focused on you.'

They watched each other intently as they walked and talked. Sometimes, a slight touch to the arm, as they pointed out a piece, made small talk of its merits.

'Why didn't you reply to my first letter?' The question was direct, hidden amongst comments about a small, bronze sculptor.

'I don't know. I waited and waited, and you

didn't contact me. I'd had such a fantastic time and…and…I suppose I was gutted that you hadn't text or phoned. I felt a fool – stupid – a bit slutty I suppose. You know, travelling all that way on a whim.'

'A whim?'

'You know what I mean. We'd only just met and here I was flying across the Atlantic to see you. When your letter finally came, I was cross, angry, remorseful.' Their eyes met. 'I should have replied. I'm sorry.'

'I'm sorry. I left the next morning – was tied up in something for a couple of weeks. It was less than thoughtless, completely unforgiveable. Please forgive me?'

'There's nothing to forgive.'

'Have you got time for something to eat? Let me buy you an early lunch?' Mina hesitated.

'Please. An hour. That's unless you have to get back to work?' Mina looked at the floor and nodded.

Later, Mina could remember little of the artwork, little of what they'd eaten or even where they'd gone. She remembered the crisp feel of his hotel sheets against her naked breasts. The way he gently and meticulously removed each piece of her clothing, her skin bristling with cold and anticipation. How she'd rubbed her fingertips across his hard chest, tracing the outline of his shoulders, feeling the taut muscles below the skin. How he'd looked at her, his eyes transfixed as he'd entered her and she took a slight involuntary intake of breath. How she'd gripped his back urgently, wanting to feel his skin on hers, his smell intoxicating. How lying there afterwards, their bodies tingling, warm and entwined, he'd whispered quietly into the silent air that he was completely and utterly in love with her.

.

17 HALLOWEEN

Lucy and Simon had never been known to throw parties of any sort, let alone fancy-dress parties. They were quiet people who worked and studied diligently, enjoying a brisk walk on a Sunday morning with the dog, followed by a latte at a local café. Since the wedding however, perhaps encouraged by its theatrical success amongst their friends, they had held a number of very successful events: a garden tea, a picnic and several, lively dinner parties. Mina, unable to attend the last one, had heard all sorts of wild stories of party games, drinking and even a suggestion of car keys in the pot – the latter she quickly dismissed as nonsense. So, when she got the email inviting her to a Halloween fancy-dress party, she wasn't surprised. What did surprise her was that Alec's name had been included on the invitation. Clearly, they had become an official item, something discussed amongst mutual friends, a relationship that had been announced to the world via the pulsating veins of the internet. They had become inseparable, their lives intrinsically entwined. He was busy always, constantly communicating with the world, often at the expense of Mina who was no longer communicating with anyone. At night, often unable to sleep, she watched him, his breathing deep. She tried to fathom the world he inhabited, both during daylight hours and drenched in slumber. As a child she had never slept well. During the day she was constantly tired, but as soon as it grew dark, her imagination intensified to the point of terror. Dark windows had to be avoided for fear of faces looking in. Under beds had to be checked and closed doors opened. Mina enjoyed the comfort of another being to share her nights, albeit one who slept well and for long periods of time. Sometimes, she mumbled quiet, sincere thoughts to him as he slept, endearments rarely reciprocated by him during daylight hours. But she knew he cared for her, wanted her. His attention was intense, compliments plentiful and he indulged her constantly. She felt like a princess in his presence – protected and adored. This was her comfort zone, her place of safety.

Several weeks had passed since meeting Daniel on that blustery, bright morning and they'd had no communication since. She'd heard through mutual friends that he was out of the country again and was glad. He confused her. She'd nurtured the guilt of their rendezvous for several days alone, unable to remove his scent and touch from her skin, too scared to face Alec in case he too could see Daniel's shadow inhabiting hers. They had made no more promises, no more plans. What they had, if anything, was mythical, exciting, and exotic. It wasn't real life. Alec, however, was ever present life and blood, available and willing. She found herself loitering each day at her flat, fussing with the cat, waiting for the post. No more letters came. No physical sign that their liaison was anything more than a teenage fumble. She gradually began to resign herself to the futility of their intimacy. Presumably he was enjoying the benefits of his nomadic lifestyle, exploring the charms of others as he traversed the world. Mina resigned herself gratefully to the life her and Alec were creating, boxing away her guilt at the indiscretion and sealing it firmly with parcel tape. She phoned and left a message thanking Lucy and Simon for the invite and saying how both her and Alec would love to come.

The night of the party was decidedly fresh and bright. The moon, fat and resplendent, sat majestically amongst the scattered stars, lighting the scene below. It was crisp and clear, children's laughter breaking the stillness as they shuffled expectantly door to door holding out their plastic buckets hoping for sweets. Mina had waited earnestly, the hallway suitably decorated with candles and webs, repeatedly opening the door to an array of miniature ghosts, witches and vampires. She loved to dress up. Halloween had been something other people celebrated when she was a child. Money had been sparse and dressing up clothes even sparser. Yet still, Mina found ways around this, a discarded dress, an old blanket, some cheap beads, all found a way into Mina's repertoire of costumes. At school, she favoured the music requiring the least fashionable attire to ensure that her daily clothing was as outlandish as possible. As a fledgling adult, she had used clothing and hair colour to mask her insecurities and give her the gall to face the world. As an adult, she immersed herself in the frivolity encapsulated and normalised by Halloween celebrations. Finally, bereft of sweets, she blew out the candles and stepped out into the chill night. Alec had yet another late business meeting and so reluctantly she'd agreed to go alone and meet him there.

Whilst others dreaded the concept of a party in drag, Mina relished it. She had boxes of wigs and bits of outfits which were regularly replenished depending on the party or event. Not every outfit was outlandish, but Mina had an instinctive ability to manipulate her outfits to create a desired effect. Tonight, was no different and she was feeling particularly pleased and self-absorbed with her outfit as she rang Lucy's doorbell. Perhaps that was why she didn't recognize Daniel as he opened the door and she shouted loudly,

'Trick or Treat?'

There was a moment of silence while she stood there grinning, waiting to be allowed in, not sure why Darth Vader wasn't stepping aside.

'Mina?' She recognized his voice instinctively, though visually he could be no other than the leader of the Dark Side.

'Daniel?' She felt nauseous. Both looked at each other awkwardly. Mina managed a further, 'Trick or treat?', her face burning beneath her make up. The silence remaining awkward.

'You look amazing…really you do.'

'Am I allowed in?'

'Sorry. Of course.' Daniel stepped aside. Behind him, an avalanche of creatures spread across Lucy and Simon's home, cobwebs swept down the staircase, lanterns hung precariously, and ghouls littered the corridor. It was suitably dark and crowded – a set of decks in the front room creating a surge of nocturnal dancing. Daniel took her hand and pulled her through the crowds into the large kitchen.

'Fancy a drink?' He shouted over the music and laughter. The kitchen was full, a gaggle of sexy witches stood in one corner gossiping, the undead dripped fake blood and various men dressed as Frankenstein attempted to drink through their rubber masks. Mina furtively surveyed the scene, hoping to find Alec, guilt swamping her body.

'Yes please. Thought you'd gone home?' She shouted over the music.

'I did. My dad's not well. Thought I'd take a couple of weeks off and come pay him a visit.'

'I'm sorry. To hear about your dad, I mean. Is he okay?'

'He's okay.' He didn't elaborate and Mina didn't feel like questioning him further. Besides, the mask was making it hard for him to talk and she could feel herself willing him to remove it so that she could see his face, his eyes, his lips. They loitered meaningful together, neither talking, neither moving away from each other.

'It seems like a good party?' She said to break the silence. 'Lots of people, hardly recognize any of them.'

'Not surprising considering the theme. I'm going to take this mask off.'

Daniel struggled to pull the hard plastic up and over his head, his soft locks electrified by the static. Mina involuntarily broke into a smile.

'Hope that's not letting the side down?' He said. 'Without the helmet I am merely a man in a black dress. By the way, you do look amazing – your own creation? '

'Partly. I'd say more of an assembly of acquired pieces, particularly the corset, was always a bit of a goth as a teenager you know – hence the ability to apply eyeliner.'

'Well, it certainly suits you.'

He took her arm, and they moved out through the French doors on to the crowded lawn. The trees strewn with colourful lanterns, sat motionless, the air still, the moon pregnant and bright. As they talked, they could see their breath, drifting vapours against the blackness. She'd forgotten how much he made her laugh, how bright his green eyes were, how long and smooth his hands.

'So, this is where you've got to.' It was Alec's voice. Mina, startled, realized that she was holding Daniel's hand, her fingers slipping quietly out of his grasp. She was glad that the night shadows disguised her embarrassment.

'Alec!' She knew her voice was a little too abrupt. 'Alec! Hi. Yes. This is Daniel. Remember? From the wedding, we were all sat together during the reception?'

'Pleased to meet you again.' Daniel said, shaking

Alec's hand enthusiastically. Mina watched as their hands gripped, fingers embraced, a long and accentuated entanglement.

'I didn't realize you two knew each other?'

'We don't really. Just from the wedding. Daniel let me in tonight...at the door...he was the one who answered the door.' She realized that she sounded guilty. Daniel however, stood relaxed and humbled.

'Right.' Alec kissed her possessively next to her mouth. 'You look fantastic.'

'Thanks – you do too'. Mina was suddenly conscious of his outfit, black spandex Batman – torso padding to accentuate his already toned chest.

'Have you both got a drink?' Both nodded, in unison.

'Well...lovely to meet you both again.' Daniel smiled broadly at them both. 'I've just noticed a couple of Stormtroopers who look like they might need their leader. Have a good evening.' And putting his mask back on, he was gone into the crowd. Alec and Mina stood quietly for a few seconds watching him go.

'You got here nice and early?'

'Why is that a problem?'

'Sorry?'

'Nothing...shall we go back inside...it's bloody freezing out here.'

They moved back into the heady heat of the house, wriggling through the creatures to get to the drinks. Their usual easy banter seemed stifled by the music, the atmosphere, and the heat. Alec, usually so attentive, seemed distant and reflective. As they stood, lonely in the crowd, drinking fizz, silent, Mina couldn't help but notice the shine of the black mask. Who it spoke to, who touched its arm coyishly, who it danced with. The more she watched, the greater the chasm between them seemed.

'I didn't realize you and that chap Daniel were friends?'

'We're not. I met him at the wedding like you.'

'You seemed to be getting on when I arrived?'

'What do you mean?'

'You seemed deep in conversation.'

'I think he felt a bit sorry for me. When I arrived, you know, by myself.'

'You said you didn't mind going alone.'

'I didn't.'

'What's the problem then?'

'I'm not sure what you mean. What's got into you?'

'Nothing. Come on let's dance.' He grabbed her hand forcefully and pulled her into the throng, not letting go. Instead, he threw her this way and that, pulling her close, holding her hard against his body and then pushing her away. Mina reacted half-heartedly. She was feeling lightheaded, the fizz making her feel a little woozy on her empty stomach and she didn't like the way he was squeezing and manipulating her. Finally, he grabbed her face, kissing her hard, his tongue invading her mouth, his teeth biting her lips. She pushed him off.

'I need some air.' Mina released herself, squirming through the crowds littering the kitchen and out into the bright coldness of the garden. She gasped as the night air hit her face frontal, goosebumps rippling along both arms. Panting, she took in long deep breaths, enjoying watching – dragon's breath her mother had always called it as they breathed hard on those cold winters' mornings walking to school. Her heart was pounding, and she wanted to be still, to be in the quiet of her own bed away from them all.

'We must stop meeting like this.' Daniel was stood in front of her, mask removed – smiling.

'Look, Daniel. I can't really do this right now. I'm with…'

'You're with that guy Alec, I know.'

'Yes, I am. I mean, we're dating.'

'You don't have to explain.'

'I know I just. Look can we just go somewhere, anywhere.'

'Now?'

'Yes, I just need to get out of here. I can't do this.'

'Okay. Where?'

'I don't care.' Mina was running, back through the crowds, the dancers, the stragglers, out on to the empty pavement. She needed to be away, somewhere else, somewhere not here. She felt lightheaded but fast, each concentrated step seemed to speed up, her legs invigorated by the coldness – her eyes focused on the pavement in front of her. Behind her, quickening footsteps and then a voice.

'Mina. Wait!'

18 WATCHING

She looked so beautiful – corseted and stockinged. Her skin soft against the metal edging, the leather gloves stopping just above the elbow, those eyes peering out beneath those dark, lined lashes. What a disaster that party had been – from start to finish. When he saw her standing there, that expression of innocence on her face; his heart had raced. He didn't want this, any of it, but he couldn't help himself. She was addictive, consuming, something he couldn't say no to, someone he couldn't be without. Yet she'd been elusive, secretive. There'd been a man with her, someone he'd briefly met at a wedding, and he didn't understand their obvious relationship. Why hadn't she mentioned it to him? Why hadn't she explained? Instead, she flitted through the evening, non-committal throughout, until finally she fled – escaped – ran. He'd had to chase her, couldn't leave her to the mercy of that freezing night, those dark streets.

Later on, in his bed, they had been cruel to each other, demanding and vicious, violating each other, pushing further and further, causing pain in order to achieve pleasure. Finally, sore and humiliated, they had lain sweaty and silent, naked, not touching, numb. He knew this was love, the frantic need to consume the other, be in their skin – but it was painful, scarring love – uncertain and desperate. In the morning when he woke, she'd gone.

19 THE BREAKUP

Nicole was worried. It had been weeks since she'd seen Mina and she'd been hearing all sorts of stories about her break up. She wouldn't answer her phone and none of their friends had seen her at any of the usual haunts. Finally, she'd woken up that morning feeling very unsettled. Her dreams had been muddled, disturbing and she knew she had to see Mina, to reassure herself that she'd not been murdered or worse, moved home with her mother.

Mina opened the door cautiously, blinking at the grey November sun, her hair, short and dishevelled hung limp across her dark-rimmed eyes. Nicole said nothing as Mina stepped back admitting her friend into the dark and musty smelling room. Nothing was awry, the room was tidy in its emptiness, the unmade bed the only clue that it was inhabited. Several bottles stood to attention in a row, their corks beheaded, a solitary glass leading the line.

'Can I?' Nicole said, indicating the curtains and Mina shrugged a reply. The light flooded the room, making the scene bleaker, colder, grey. She forced a crack in the sash window and gulped the cold air deeply, preparing to plunge herself back into the stale atmosphere of the room. Mina sat deflated on the edge of the bed, limp, doll-like; her eyes glazed and expressionless. Nicole sat next to her, placing one arm around her friend's shoulder and pulling her head in close.

'Why didn't you say something? Oh Mina.' The sobs began slowly, silently, short shudders, her face pressed hard against Nicole's chest. Then the convulsions started, great spasms, uncontrollable and rhythmic, accompanied by deep guttural moans. Nicole held her fast, resisting Mina's contractions, her chest and neck wet with tears and snot, her fingers gripping the back of Mina's sweater. Finally, they resided, slowing, becoming shallower, short judders and sniffs. Nicole lay her down on the bed and pulled a blanket over her coiled body. Sensing movement, the cat stirred from its slumber and began to knead them both, its purring loud, its pawing pedantic and persistent.

In the kitchen, on the worktop, a pair of discarded scissors and the shards of her cut hair lay abandoned and forlorn next to an open tin of cat food and several empty bottles of pills. Nicole returned quickly to the prostrate Mina, curled foetal-like, under the scratchy blanket.

'Did you take these?' She said, shoving the empty bottles at her. Mina, sore eyes closed protectively, breathing raspy and wet, stayed motionless.

'Mina?'

'They've all gone.' She whispered, barely

audible. 'All of them, all gone.'

Nicole dialled the number, slowly stroking the clumps of Mina's hair as she did so.

'Ssh. It's going to be ok. You're going to be ok. Try and stay awake for me now, ok?'

Gently, Mina softly cried, while Nicole strained to hear the welcoming sound of sirens arriving at the door.

20 THE AFTERLIFE

Mina lay prostrate and motionless in the iron bed, disguised by starched, clinical sheets and identified by a number on her bracelet. Three other young women shared her room, paper curtains demarcating their territories, a medical boarding school for those mentally challenged, those not trusted to survive in the real world. Two orderlies had held her down, forced a pipe down her throat and filled her belly with activated charcoal, foie-gras style, again and again while her body revolted, spasmed, convulsed and finally excreted the poison she'd lovingly given it. She'd fought hard, her arms flaying, her chest heaving, as they bound her arms to the bed. Finally, exhausted and spent, her throat on fire, she'd given in, allowed them to strip her naked, wash her and commit her to this bed. They wanted her to talk, to explain, to confess, to plead guilty to her crimes. Mina, full of self-loathing had nothing to say, nothing to admit to. They'd called her mother, against her wishes and she'd arrived, sat stone-faced and expectantly next to the bed, waiting for answers. There were none. There was nothing to say. So, the stand-off continued. Silent days went by whilst a succession of experts sat and listened to Mina's mother describe her perfect childhood and Mina stayed inside. Mina stayed inside. Mina stayed inside where it was quiet and calm, and she could think. Her lips, dry and ragged, were steadfast – they refused to open. They refused nourishment. They refused to talk. No friends were allowed, too upsetting. No messages from the outside world. So, Mina stayed inside and played with her thoughts of tents and bridges and lightening and sunsets and flesh and him.

Then one day, through the fog in her head, she heard words, an offer, a sojourn at her mother's house, they thought it might do her good. She listened hard, it was difficult to hear their voices, muffled, echoing in her head, a long way away, but yes, her mother was offering to take her home. Mina twitched. She opened her mouth. She tried to mouth a word, but nothing came out. Then, in the distance, she heard a whispered 'no'. It was very faint, and she wasn't sure whether or not it had actually come from her – so she tried again and listened. They looked at her, startled initially, quiet, expectant. So, she tried again – to please them – to see them smile, 'no' – timid and faint. They checked her chart, fetched another, whispered amongst themselves. Her mother smiling down at her, said 'Good girl. Good girl', like she used to do to the puppy when it had wet on the newspaper just inside the back door. Mina suddenly felt very tired.

21 CHRISTMAS

The wet December weather was playing havoc with the media's portrayal of Christmas. On TV, families threw snowballs, went to sparkling cocktail parties and gathered nostalgically around laden trees, smiling adoringly and giving small, immaculately wrapped gifts. Mina, curled cat-like in the chair, watched with disdain. Outside, the monotonous tepid rain dampened Christmas cheer, forcing last-minute shoppers to dodge between puddles, battle with umbrellas and endure deliberate queues. It was needlessly mild and insipid, irritating. Mina took comfort in this misery, the isolation it caused, the lack of jollity. At night, lying flat on her teenage bed, she listened intently to the repetitive patter on the Velux window above. She saw the small girl of her childhood, cocooned in her sleeping bag on a made-up bed in a holiday caravan; the rain persistent and reliable, the comforting memory faded and blurred. The holiday itself is distant, just the warmth in the van, the velour seating, the compact kitchen, the mock fireplace, the wet journeys to the toilet block in wellies and PJs. The pennies for the arcade, the coins used to buy bottled milk and pop. Lying once again under her mother's roof, the warmth gone, Mina waits, waits for the void to be filled, the emptiness subsumed, the pause button to be stopped. It's a long wait, the days and nights smudged, indistinct. She picks at food, sleeps, watches TV, sleeps. Her mother seems happy, focused, attentive and purposeful. Mina watches with hate from the side-lines. Years she'd spent trying to get away and one flick of the wrist and the cord springs her back to GO without picking up £200. There is smiling bustle around her prostrate mind. Decorations go up, food and drink are stock-piled, deliberations are had over gifts and phone calls made. Flying snowmen, animated Santa's and white Christmases play on a constant loop, their reds and whites flashing across the screen, distorted against the gold trimmings and polished crystal, the neatly placed bowls of nuts and Quality Street. Mina, shorn and bruised, sits silently, waiting to heal – waiting for this incarceration to be over. In the chair opposite, her dad sits silently too, resigned to his solitude, happy in the world his mind has created undemanding. Friends had called, been fielded, their best wishes noted and relayed, no visitors allowed on doctors' orders. It is this control she likes, thinks Mina.

Finally, Christmas Day arrives. Neighbours drop by for a sherry and an ogle at the girl undone. 'She was always a bit full of herself, a bit wild' they think. 'It'll do her good to be back with her mother for a bit – reign her in'. Mina performs appropriately, her mother sat next to her on the armrest, hand squeezing tightly on her shoulder, warning, slight smile and nod at relevant times. Then lunch for the three of them, carols on the radio, consumption, paper hats and trifle. Water in a wine glass, 'It's for the best Mina – you heard what the doctor said about mixing the drugs and wine', chocolate and TV. Mother is pleased with Mina's performance, feels a corner has been turned, says so to father as he sleeps in the chair. Mina feels like she is at the end of a very long tunnel, the scene happening in the distance, she is watching her body act out the scenario. It is quiet noisy, echoey and muffled. Her head is blurred – dense – misty – she just wants to sleep and be still.

22 THE ESCAPE PLAN

'I promise I will look after her – she won't be out of my sight for a minute.'

'I'm not sure about this Nicole – it isn't part of her recovery plan you know.'

'She'll be fine. It'll do her good – see some old friends – get some fresh air.'

The weather had finally delivered a sparse scattering of frost, much to the relief of Nicole who couldn't take another day of being cooped up with her future in-laws in their overcrowded house in North London. Using Mina as an escape, she'd arrived first thing, gifts in hand, offering to take her out for an hour's 'sale' shopping. Mina, allowed herself to be washed, dressed and bundled out of the front door, compliant to the demands of both women. Once safely ensconced in a seat on the tube, her hand held tightly, both women began to relax. Mina found herself transfixed by the map, mentally ticking off the stations, the mistiness beginning to dissolve, her eyes beginning to open.

'I bloody hate Christmas. Awful time. Endless hours of banal conversation and food.' Nicole stopped and looked quickly at Mina. One solitary tear was rolling across her cheek. Nicole wiped it quickly and squeezed her hand tight.

'It'll be ok. I promise. I won't leave you there.' She whispered. 'Come on – it's our stop next.'

Nicole had no intention of shopping. Instead, she'd arranged a small gathering of the festival girls at a bistro bar in Camden. On the way, they'd dropped in to a mutual friend's salon and as a Christmas gift, Nicole paid for Mina to have her chopped hair controlled and a smudge of eyeliner applied. The result was extremely pleasing and even Mina couldn't help but smile timidly when she saw her reflection in the mirror.

'Not bad girl – not bad at all.' Nicole stood proudly behind her. 'You look fab Mina.'

'Thank you.'

'Ssh. Come on. Lunch is waiting.'

'You know…for everything.'

The bistro was small and empty when they arrived. A couple of waitresses dawdling by the till, stopped chatting reluctantly to point them in the direction of a round table near the back of the room. Nicole, ignoring Mina's pleas, ordered a bottle of wine and two glasses as they ambled across the deserted room.

'Have you been here before?' Mina whispered, reluctant to break the quiet. One waitress arrived to light the candle perched in the middle of the table, while the other nonchalantly switched on some South American music, a welcome relief from the Christmas fayre both girls had come to hate.

'Don't be put off. The food is amazing, and it

gets really busy. You'll see. We're just a little early.' Mina scanned the décor, predictable ceiling fans, candles and an array of artefacts, all attempting to add atmosphere to a run-down North London building. The wine arrived, and Mina was surprised at how good it tasted after so many weeks forced abstaining. She swallowed the first glass and Nicole poured her the second.

'Has it been really awful?' Nicole eyed her sympathetically. Mina didn't meet her eyes.

'You know…difficult. Have you been checking in on?'

'Yes, he's fine. Eating well. Persecuting the neighbourhood cats. All the usual. Don't worry about him Mina – he's fine.'

'Thank you.'

'For what?'

'You know. Everything.'

'Listen Mina. You don't have to thank me. I didn't do anything. We're friends, ok?'

'I know but.'

'No buts. You'd do the same for me. You know you would. Besides, I haven't quite rescued you yet have I? How am I going to get you out of the grasp of mummy? You have a five o'clock curfew today!'

'I dunno.'

'We have to get you well. Get you back out there living again. When do you have to go back to the doctors?'

'Next week. Final decision. Can I do it alone?' Nicole took her hand and looked at her straight.

'Of course, you can. We can do this.' The door

opened, and the others joined them, their enthusiasm and excitement at seeing Mina overwhelming. Her newly cropped hair was admired, Christmas horror stories swapped, and a great quantity of wine and tapas ordered. Mina, though feeling lightheaded and overwhelmed, began to breathe again, to notice the world around her. As the Bistro filled, so did Mina's spirits. She looked at her three friends, teasing each other, laughing and giggling over the mundane and the trivial. They seemed more alive than she'd ever seen them, happy. The two waitresses, now flushed and busy, darted in and around the tables, delivering little plates of delicacies and smiling dutifully as they worked on their tips. The food was spicy and steaming and the girls chatted incessantly as they passed the little plates around, dishing out little portions and sharing hunks of garlic bread. 'Leftovers', her mother would have called this food and Mina smiled quietly to herself. Finally, coffee finished, they ordered a bottle of fizz.

'A toast to the New Year.' Nicole proclaimed loudly, annoying a group of Chinese tourists sat on the adjacent table.

'To the New Year.' They chorused, clinking glasses and giggling. Mina grabbed Nicole's hand under the table. 'Thank you' she mouthed again and looked at her friends gratefully.

23 A BRIEF ENCOUNTER

He hadn't expected to see her. Didn't recognize her at first. The dark, shiny hair, cut short, pixie-like against her pale skin. He was with Susan, walking back from the Sunday market, when she stopped to do up the lace on her boots. Through the steamy glass he'd watched in awe the four faces laughing over the champagne flutes. It had taken a while to register Mina, cloistered close to Nicole. She seemed fragile, smaller than he remembered her, reticent.

'I'm just going to get a bottle of water. Do you want anything?'

'No thanks. I'll wait here for you.' He stood, transfixed, staring across the darkened room at the table of young women, his woman. She was quiet, listening intently to Nicole telling a story, her eyes following each hand movement, each facial expression. She looked thinner, perhaps because her mane of hair wasn't flowing voluptuously across each shoulder, her neck slimmer, longer. He hadn't seen her since Halloween. She'd not returned his calls. Her friends appeared sworn to secrecy and there was no sign of her at her flat. The last couple of months had been hard. His father had passed, and he'd been engrossed in sorting out the financial affairs. Day after day, he dealt with solicitors and accountants. Night after night he'd waited outside Mina's flat, hoping, praying for a glimpse. Sometimes, he was fooled into believing the silhouette at the window was Mina rather than her friend Nicole, who he quickly realized was feeding the cat. He'd never experienced such hopelessness, such insurmountable anguish. Though a traveller by nature, he felt rooted to this small plot, unable to detach himself from the seemingly barren soil. While every fibre of his being wanted to run, he felt paralysed by grief and fear. 'Fuck' he thought, not managing to remove his gaze from her petite face, 'fuck you'. But he knew he didn't mean it.

'Ready?' He turned, startled to see Susan smiling expectantly at him. He'd met her at a Christmas party and they'd had a couple of mediocre dates since. Standing there now, he felt suddenly guilty, like he was cheating, like he had to move Susan away in case Mina came out and saw them, caught them. He felt flustered and there was an unrecognizable tightness in his chest.

'Yes, of course. Why wouldn't I be?'

'Sorry?' He took her arm and quickly they crossed the high street, and he began to march purposefully towards the tube.

'Hey! What's the rush? Wait up.' He wanted to slow down but couldn't, terrified that Mina would see him, would want to talk to him, would make him feel what he'd worked so hard to suppress. 'Wait!' He stopped and reluctantly turned. Around him the bustle of shoppers tutted, elbows shoved, and bags thrashed against his hips.

'Look, I'm sorry, I don't feel well. I might have to go home. I'm sorry. Can I call you tomorrow? Will you be ok getting home?' He felt like he was going to throw up. He needed to be alone, away from the increasing surge of tourists.

'Of course. Are you ok? You've gone very pale!'

'I'm fine. I'll phone you tomorrow. OK?' He was gone. Subsumed into the crowd of Sunday shoppers, inconsequential, hidden.

For a while, Susan watched him go, then turned – walking back to the bustle of the market – theatrically unimpressed and determined not to waste any more shopping time.

24 THE ESCAPE

'There's a man at the door for you Mina!' Her mother stood incredulous, her defences destroyed by the downright cheek of a man knocking on her door at nine o'clock at night, when she was dressed and ready for bed. 'He won't tell me his name and he's refused to leave. Shall I call the police?'

'The police?'

'Well, I can't be having strangers...men, knocking at this time of night – especially when you are in this frail condition. And he won't leave. Your father's useless – he's refusing to come to the door. How do I know what that man wants.'

'Mother, has he threatened you?'

'He says he wants to speak to you and he won't leave until you come to the door. I won't have it Mina – whilst you're under my roof – you're not bringing men home.'

'How can I have brought men home...I've been in for weeks.'

'So why is he here?'

'I don't know.' The doorbell rang again – persistent and prolonged.

'Get the phone.'

'You are not calling the police mother. Don't be ridiculous. Let me go and throw some jeans on. Tell him I'll be down in a minute.'

'I'm not going to the door again. He might force his way through – then where would we be? He might kill us all!'

'Mother!' Quickly, Mina sprang upstairs, ruffled her hair and slid into some jeans and a baggy pullover. Cautiously she peeped out of the upstairs window, but could only see the top of his head, hidden in the shadows, the porch light switched off by her mother who was by now convinced they were all about to be murdered. She sat on the top step, listening to her mother berate her father in the front room and waited. Whoever it was, she wasn't sure she was ready.

'Mina? Are you in there?' His voice instantly sent shivers running down her spine. 'Mina? I'm not going without seeing you.' Quietly she tiptoed down the stairs – a child hiding – playing. She stood silently, listening, her fingertips braced on the door. 'Mina?' She sensed his insistence. 'Mina, I mean it, I will stay here all night if necessary.' Tentatively she opened the door and peeped out.

Alec stood there, an enormous bunch of white lilies across his arm, his face masked by the dark. She stepped out on the porch, closing the door behind her and stood in front of him, arms clasped protectively around her body.

'Oh Mina.' He reached up and touched her hair, pulling her head gently towards his chest. She allowed herself to be pulled into his embrace and he wrapped his big coat over her narrow shoulders to protect her from the icy wind.

'Come on baby. Let's take you home.' And laying the lilies at the front door he cradled her to the waiting car and helped her get in.

25 THE DISAPPEARANCE

'What do you mean she's gone?'

'She's gone! Left! A bunch of lilies left in her place.' Nicole tried to gather her thoughts, understand what was happening. She'd rarely spoken to Mina's mother let alone at ten o'clock at night during a family crisis. 'Do you think I should call the police...perhaps I should have done it when he first knocked.'

'When who first knocked? I'm sorry – I'm a little confused. Tell me what happened again.'

'I don't know. It's all become a blur. Some stranger. A man. Knocked on the door at nine o'clock!'

'Yes. You said that.'

'So, I reluctantly went to the door. Which was bad enough because I don't normally go to the door at that time of night, especially as I was in my night things. I mean, who knocks on a door at nine o'clock! Anyway, he refused to leave unless Mina came to the door...was very insistent...got almost aggressive with me...shouting her name through the door. So, I said no. I told him I would call the police. I threatened him. Perfectly within my right to do so. But he wouldn't listen. Kept calling her name loudly through the door. Clearly woke the whole street! So, she went to the door. I told her not to. Said I would call the police. But would she listen? The next thing I hear is screeching tyres and she's gone! Manhandled into a car no doubt – forced away by some trafficker!'

'I'm sure it's someone that she knows. She wouldn't have answered the door otherwise.' Nicole tried to convince herself, her brain desperately going through the likely scenarios.

'You don't know that, Nicole. She's been in a very fragile state...a very fragile state and now this! I should have phoned the police. I know I should have. I only phoned you because I thought you might know something. You know some of these men she used to hang around with. I thought you might be able to reassure me.'

'No. Like I said. I haven't seen her since our day out. We've spoken a couple of times on the phone but nothing else.'

'Well did she mention anything? Any men that she knows. Any plans?'

'Why would she? She's been happy over the last couple of weeks.' Nicole lied, her mind trying to work out whether he'd come back. How he knew where her mother lived.

'I mean, she can't be safe out there alone; prey to anyone.'

'I'm sure she's fine. There's no need to call the police. It's bound to be someone she knows, someone she wants to be with. I'm sure she'll phone.' Nicole lied again. It was becoming a habitual habit. 'Besides, he brought her flowers, didn't he?'

'Yes. Lilies. White lilies. Why leave them then – abandoned outside the front door?'

'Were they discarded or placed?'

'I don't know. Does it matter? Really? Placed I think, why?'

'Well, it shows there wasn't a struggle doesn't it. Look don't do anything stupid. I'll phone a couple of friends. See if anyone's heard anything. Ok?'

'Is it stupid to worry about your only daughter? In her present state, I think I should just call the police.'

'No, of course it's not stupid, but just let me see what I can find out. I'll phone you back if I hear anything.' The third lie – I really must stop this Nicole thought.

'I appreciate this, Nicole. I didn't know who else to turn to and you know she can be headstrong – giddy – unpredictable. She's worried me lately. She's herself but not, if you know what I mean. Somehow more extreme, more prone to being impulsive. It's a good job term hasn't started yet. What will we say to her headmaster if she doesn't turn up for work?' So, she hasn't shared that important piece of information, thought Nicole. She hasn't disclosed her lack of work and money.

'It'll be fine…we'll sort it…I promise.' This was also becoming a habit thought Nicole, promising the female members of this family, that everything was going to be alright. 'I'll phone as soon as I find anything out…try and get some rest.'

Putting down the phone, Nicole sighed. It felt somehow disloyal to hunt down her friend when clearly, her friend wanted to disappear for a while, escape, heal. Yet, what if she was in danger. What if she had gone against her will. The thought sounded ridiculous as she said it and she was pleased no police had been called. Who to call was the question. She didn't want to start phoning random friends, only to vociferously spread the news of Mina's disappearance. Instead, she thought she'd visit her flat in the morning. See if by any chance she was there. See if she'd taken any clothes. Nicole still had keys, was visiting regularly to feed the cat so would know whether or not Mina had been there. The plan seemed feasible and would give Nicole something to do, an action, something tangible that would stop her and Mina's mother worrying about sex trafficking and murder. What was the worst that could happen? She'd walk in on their naked bodies.

26 A NEW BEGINNING

Mina woke in the early hours, thirsty and restless. Pinioned by Alec's arm moulded around her torso she felt hot and sweaty. Carefully, so as not to wake him, she slowly prised each part of her body free until she was able to sit naked on the edge of his large bed. It was dark and still, the moon hidden by a veil of cloud, emitting a diluted chink of light through the partially closed shutters. She fumbled amongst the pile of clothes, hastily discarded on the bedroom floor, before giving up and heading for the ensuite bathroom.

Sitting astride the toilet, squinting under the neon lights, Mina felt serene and still. She knew she should call her mother at some point, knew she'd be worried and distraught, but couldn't quite conceive what she would say to her. 'Hi mum – I'm fine – see you Sunday'. Or 'so sorry – shouldn't have left like that but you drive me insane'. Hard to quantify that one considering recent events she supposed. 'Sorry mum – desperate to feel a man's arms around me'. There were no words that could appropriately capture what she'd done or why. Best therefore, not to say anything at all. Or so she reasoned. She looked at the huge white bath sat majestically in the centre of the room and felt a sudden urge to slip under the cover of warm, scented suds. Wiping herself, she stood and examined her face in the large mirror over the sinks. Her eyes, still dark and potent, were framed by dark circles and she saw the enforced incarceration in her mother's house, in the fragments of fine lines in the corners of her eyes. Finding a bottle of water, she gulped its contents, gasping as she completed the task, wiping the drips with her bare arms. She looked at her erect nipples and the spread of goosebumps covering her torso. She suddenly realized that she was cold, her eyes felt heavy, and she needed to sleep in the cocoon provided by his hairy body. She switched off the light and fumbled her way out into the darkness. She could hear his soft breathing, see his gentle face silhouetted against the white pillows as she slipped in to the warm bed, wrapping her arms around his waist. Entwined, she stroked the soft down of his belly, circling, dipping her fingers in and out of the soft space of his belly button. Each circle, her fingers trickled lower and lower finding his thick, coarse hair and the emerging flesh beginning to throb in its prostrate state. She scooped it into her palm and began to gently caress and kneed between her fingers and thumb as it pulsed and enlarged. Alec stirred – somewhere between slumber and consciousness, he turned his body to confront her. But she pushed him gently on to his back, eased him a little into her and pausing briefly to present her throbbing nipples into his open mouth, she sat down, taking him completely, feeling him expand and fill her.

27 THE HUNT FOR ANSWERS

By Friday, having not heard from Mina, Nicole was at the point of calling the police herself. She felt annoyed. Annoyed at the responsibility placed on her and her friend's lack of consideration. She'd had to endure countless, pointless conversations with Mina's mother and was being sucked into the whole conspiracy theory of mad men and traffickers. If this wasn't enough, Sampson, the man she thought she loved, was acting like a spoilt child. On top of a full day of teaching she'd had to drive to the next manor, to retrieve him from his friends and several whiskey chasers. Enough is enough she thought as she walked the final hundred yards to Mina's flat to feed the blessed cat. However, as she turned the corner and saw the large 'To Let' sign protruding violently outside the front door, her annoyance became reluctant anger. She was seething by the time she put the key into the lock and opened the door onto the emptiness within. It was gone. Everything stripped bare, the humanity shrivelled, merely a couple of shoddy looking rooms with bare pipe work and some interesting mouldy corners. Even the cat had gone. Its smell the only reminder that it had ever been there. She'd begun to respect the wily creature as it resigned itself to different caretakers, principally Nicole, throughout Mina's numerous absents. Nicole sighed heavily. The flat seemed smaller naked. Shrivelled and unloved. Nicole sat in the windowsill, picking at the fraying peony wallpaper. At least Mina was okay she thought, well alive enough to recruit an estate agent. And at least she now had something to report to the mother, no violent bodily crime had taken place. Yet the growing sense of betrayal jerked inside and began to smother her otherwise calm demeanour. She walked into the tiny kitchenette, recoiling at the stagnant odour of milk long warmed. Next to the sink was an envelope with her name on it.

My dearest friend,
Thank you for everything you have done for me.
You saved my life, and I will always be grateful.
Alec and I are going to give it another go – cat and
all! I have to give it a try, besides, the rent hasn't
been paid for a while…I presume you will have had
grief from mother – sorry! I love you Nicole –
always - will be in touch soon.
Mina xxx

Nicole crumpled the paper in her grasp, stared absently out of the window for a moment, before shutting the door on the flat and her friend.

28 THE WORLD ACCORDING TO ALEC

It didn't take long for Mina to relax into the world according to Alec. The year was almost at an end and consequently their intertwined lives were filled with shopping, dinners and champagne. Mina's recent period of convalescence and the incident necessitating it, hadn't been discussed since that first night together. Their breakup following the Halloween party had been civilized, discussed as a necessary solution to the growing chasm between them. The reason for the chasm, while suspected by Alec, had not been. Her emotional free-fall and smash Mina's honesty on this first night back together felt cathartic. He listened attentively, his eyes not leaving hers, intermittently nodding. When she'd finished, he'd remained silent, pulling her gently towards him. He held her tightly, stroking her hair like she was a child, returned from an escapade in the woods, needing rescue and comfort. The comfort of his chest rising and falling, his heart beating in time with hers, stilled the muffled tears. This was her comfort zone, she knew that now, this was where she was supposed to be. Rescued again, she allowed herself to be nurtured and treasured.

Mina had collected her belongings from the flat the following day, hastily shoving the pile of official post deep into her suitcase. The cat, pleased to see a human face, went with her willingly. The letting agent seemed relieved when Mina told him that she'd vacated the property, reminding her that she could forget her deposit and that she had thirty days in which to pay the arrears. She felt guilty for not contacting her mother and even more so for the hastily written note left for Nicole's benefit. However, Alec's persistent reasoning had helped her see that a few days distance from her friends and parents, would aid her resolve if anyone tried to change her mind. Not that they would. Mina felt protected and adored. Alec kept her close and busy. Mina found herself an attentive and grateful recipient, childlike in her acceptance of his gifts, time and attention.

As they sat cocooned in the taxi, her hand securely cupped in his, Mina pushed the overwhelming sense of panic deep into her bowel and tried to concentrate on breathing. She looked out onto the neon-bright world of central London, the hordes of merry-makers streaming to unknown places, parties and events. She felt stifled and self-conscious in her outfit, wary of their destination. Alec leaned over and gently kissed the side of her exposed neck. She involuntarily shivered. He smiled, the gentle creases around his eyes softening and reassuring.

'The shape of your mouth I could probably draw by heart.' He said and then kissed her tenderly. Mina felt the knot in her stomach dissolve, and she kissed him back.

The party was a corporate event, dinner and dancing amidst strangers that neither of them knew well. Alec spent much of the evening steering Mina around the room to meet business acquaintances and associates. Mina smiled appropriately, listened to their chatter and nibbled cautiously at the plentiful supply of food and champagne. By eleven o'clock, isolated and bored, she was relieved when Alec suggested that they leave.

Outside, the cold air confronted Mina's naked flesh and though she shivered, she embraced long, deep breaths of the fresh night air.

'Let's walk. It's not that far' Mina smiled and nodded. Alec removed his jacket and covered her shoulders, pulling her in, protectively close. 'I'm sorry…this evening was dull'.

'It's fine…it was nice…I enjoyed it.'

'You sure?' Alec laughed, pulling her in closer. They walked in contented silence amidst the taut anticipation of the end of the year. The bank of the Thames was littered with excited couples and families, some in sparkly frocks and heals, others in woollen hats and thick jackets. All united in their eagerness to countdown the old and welcome in the new. All enroute to some predetermined place, a party or parade or spectacle. In contrast, Mina and Alec meandered, their footsteps in tandem, their bodies entwined. The sparkling city effervescent, outdoing the luminescent moon above, the meagre collection of stars watching patiently in the sky. Mina peeked out from the collar of Alec's jacket, watching smiling faces as they passed, catching glimpses of conversation. Neither spoke, content in the crowds; unified.

'Stay here a moment. I won't be long'. Mina, obedient, waited outside the thronged bar, aloof and interested. The windows steamy, bodies loitering outside, sparkle and stilettoes littering the crowd. Laughter penetrated the excited bustle and packs jostled territorially for space on the crowded pavement. Mina found herself backing against a wall, blending into the shadows deliberately to avoid being knocked, accosted or dripped on. In a doorway, a mangled head sat atop a bundle of rags, morbidly still and silent. Cardboard clearly marked this home, a collection of plastic bags its décor and a grasped Café Nero cup the only sign of life. Blackened fingers, their tips yellow and calloused, warmed themselves on the steaming cup. A meagre assortment of copper sat pitifully on a greasy chip plate, the pennies too few to count, charred and dull. Mina, felt in Alec's pocket, pulling out some coins, shiny and solid, she rubbed them between her fingers, trying to fathom her next move, decide whether to speak or drop and run.

'There you are. You okay?'

'Of course,' she said, pushing the coins back into the dark recesses of his coat pocket.

Alec, smiling, aimed a large bottle in her direction, twirling two glasses between his fingers. 'Difficult to get hold of tonight…come on.'

On the bridge they stopped midway, leaning

over, gazing into the blackness of the cold water below. Crowds thronged past them, the bubbling of anticipation growing as each minute pulsed. Alec fumbled to release the cork, finally spewing it out into the darkness of the river as the first bangs hit the darkness, showering the London sky with avalanches of glitter and light. Huge jellyfishes of colour exploded and disintegrated, followed by a frenzy of shots, bullets flying silently upwards and cascading silver, pinks and gold downwards onto the upturned faces. Around them people cheered, kissed, and sang, the noise impenetrable, the darkness awash with crystal and lights, car horns blaring.

'Will you marry me?'

'What?' Mina, consumed by the spectacle, grinning, looked up into Alec's sincere eyes.

'Will you marry me?' He said again, quieter this time, expectant. Mina's smile disappeared. She knew what she was meant to do, how she was meant to react, but her face, always unforgiving, betrayed her. Alec, crest-fallen, stared out into the now quiet darkness. Mina reached for his arm, fingertips loitering on his shirt sleeve.

'I just need to…to think…I didn't expect, I mean…I had no idea. I mean it is all very sudden. Alec! Please look at me…please.' His body turned at right angles, he swigged back the glass and poured himself another.

'It's fine…shit it was a stupid notion anyway…I just, you know…thought we were getting on…working. Christ. I love you…it's mad I know. I just do.'

Mina quietly reached up and kissed him, soft and tenderly, their lips still wet from the sweet champagne.

'Let's go home, shall we?'

29 THE NEW YEAR

Daniel was in good spirit. It was the start of a new year and he felt bloated with optimism and resolutions. The party last night had been good, his sister's friends particularly attentive and a morning in bed, followed by a brisk run, restorative. He'd chosen this spot to meet, purely for location and convenience; somewhere within walking distance should he decide to abort and return to his bed. As it was, the sun seemed intent on permeating its way through the clouds, so he decided to brave the chill January air and take his coffee outside. Quietly he watched as the world ambled, lost in gentle thought of the last few days and his impending flight home. He loved being in London with his sister and friends. Loved the opportunities presented by the diversity of the landscape. Loved the anonymity of the big city and the intimacy of familiar streets and faces. Hoped that Mina's face might be there amongst them. He knew the futile longing for something gone, long gone. But also knew that the unattainable was what gripped him, hence his job. As a small boy he had always wanted the unavailable, the toy that had sold out, the horse that was too big for him to ride. As an adult, this had continued. He deliberately chose work not assigned to him, visited places not deemed as safe and grabbed at interviews no one would give. Mina was no different. She was not his, not safe and definitely not contactable. However, he couldn't wrench out the feeling deep within him, that she was his and that he wanted to make her safe.

'Hi.'

'Oh hi.' Daniel jumped up, knocking his coffee, a kerfuffle of movement and elaborate social kissing. 'I wasn't sure you'd come.'

'Why?' Susan smiled, and Daniel remembered how her face shone. 'You asked me'.

'I know…that doesn't always mean things go to plan. What can I get you?'

'What are you having?'

'Coffee – well what's left of it. Shall we have something to toast the New Year?' She nodded, squeezing around the narrow table, to sit on the metal chair. She smelt of hand-made soap and freshness. Her large cable jumper swamped by a layer of azure blue, the colour of her eyes, she seemed perfectly at ease in the early afternoon sunlight, bright and relaxed. He remembered her pale naked skin, the shape of her lower spine and had to squirm onto another leg to avoid his urges becoming visible. The waitress, clearly adept at avoiding all idling conversation, returned with two glasses of prosecco.

'How was your family gathering last night?' He was determined to keep the conversation light…consistent.

'So…so…you know what these things are like – too much alcohol – high expectations – mass disappointment. No rows…which is exceptional – everyone was on their best behaviour for some reason. How about you – you were with your sister weren't you?'

'Yes. Amazing how annoying she was as a child and how interesting she's become as an adult. I can honestly say I quite enjoy her company, especially after dad and such.'

'Look don't take this the wrong way ok…but how long are you here for?'

'Another couple of days tops…back to work I'm afraid.'

'I'm not prying – just interested really.'

'It's weird. When I'm there I love it. When I'm here, I worry that I shouldn't be going back to there. Stupid I know.'

'It's not stupid at all. London is your home'

'Yes, but unfortunately, it's not. I grew up here, but my adult life is wherever work takes me.' The sun, braver now, was beaming. Daniel stretched his legs out in front, his chin tilted upwards into the shaft of light that was illuminating her blond bob. They'd met, fumbled and fell into a couple of dinner dates. She was intelligent, gentle and funny. He liked her company, liked being touched, liked her simplicity. She understood the situation, his impermanence, the expected brevity of their friendship, if that's what it was.

'Isn't it beautiful by the water. I come here as often as I can.'

Daniel, perfectly relaxed, stretched across and lifted the tips of her pink fingers, his lips just brushing their ends. Her eyes, azure gems, held his gaze briefly, the corners of her mouth slightly lifted. He noticed one tiny indentation, a burgeoning smile crease, a slight imperfection in an otherwise perfect face. Momentarily, neither said anything. Then a shiver raced vertically up her back and she gently trembled. Their locked gaze broke, and Daniel moved his head, conscious of a slight stiffness from this morning's run. Then he paused sharply, hand still stroking the back of his neck. A dark familiar head was moving through the crowds towards them. He couldn't be sure. Had to be sure. His heart was pounding, beads of sweat broke on his forehead He dropped her hand and sat rigid.

'Are you ok?' He couldn't speak. The hairs on his chest and arms were alive with static electricity – tingling and moist. 'Daniel? Are you ok?'

'Um…yes…just…it's nothing.' He wished people would move out of the way. His eyes darted, scanning, searching through the throng of people. Why couldn't he see? He wanted to stand so that he could see better, but he could feel his companion's critical eyes.

'Daniel? Can I get you something? Water?'

'Yes, no, sorry, I'm fine – really, I am fine.' He tried to soften the tone of his voice, but instead, his usually deep voice betrayed him in an ever so slightly shrill. He couldn't take his eyes off the crowd, squinting, straining, looking for that dark hair and those eyes. Then there she was. Real life. Strolling as bold as brash towards him. She was alone, confidently sweeping her way along the towpath, causing the crowds to spontaneously part as she glided through. Her hair, shorter than he remembered it, framed her contented expression. She hadn't seen him, wasn't aware of anyone around her, was purposefully aiming for a planned destination and designated time.

In the distance, foggy and disjointed, Daniel could hear fragments of a woman's voice, 'Are you ok…you've gone very pale…Daniel are you listening'. But the sound of his quickened breathing, her feet coming towards him and the pounding in his head, obliterated any sense of reality, of real time. His chest felt tight as he contemplated what he should do, what he would say. He could almost smell her…taste her. He felt a cold hand on his brow and convulsed, snapping back, his eyes refocusing on the face an inch from his, the furrowed brows and concerned expression.

'Daniel! It's me…are you ok? You went very pale…is there something I can get you? He stood quickly, craning his neck, stretching his body high to follow her final moments before she disappeared into a car, and he was left in the cold brutality of his loneliness. He smiled, trying to reassure both of them that he hadn't lost himself completely, knowing full well that they wouldn't see each other again. Knowing full well that he had scared her again, his emotional absence a concern to those living in the real world. While she stared bemused, Daniel realized what he had to do in order to survive – flight would not be an option this time. He reached for his phone and quickly dialled his boss in New York.

30 THE DECISION

'Yes,' She'd said without thinking as she got into his car. 'I'll marry you'. Alec looked at her, his eyebrow slightly raised.

'But you said…'

'I know…I just, I just sometimes need time, you know, to adjust to things – get them straight in my head.' She smiled convincingly, her eyes not meeting his as he joined the Sunday lunchtime traffic queues.

The early evening light punctured the soft clouds, warming her down-turned face. His smile pleased, relieved, beamed across the small veranda.

'Why the change of heart?'

'What?'

'The change of heart…you know…the no…then the yes…your decision?'

'I just…well…you know…' Mina smiled, deliberately coquettishly and convincingly. 'I love you…want to be with you…was just a bit surprised when you asked. You know…not been back together long. Was concerned. Found it difficult to cope with our breakup. Didn't want to repeat it again.'

'Come here!' He ordered, patting the arm of his chair and she moved dutifully, his clasping arm circulating, his grip firm.

'I was beginning to think you'd say no – then where would we be?' Mina stroked his forehead with her free arm and kissed his upturned face.

'Don't be silly. Why wouldn't I marry you, my wonderful man.' She lay her head against his shoulder and he stroked her back with his broad hand.

It had been a strange day, a disturbing one for Mina. She'd woken before dawn, flushed and tearful. The midnight proposal and the ensuing silent walk home had tested her nerve, the mettle she believed she possessed. Instead of feeling relieved, finally in control, within a finger's breath of plan B, she'd felt blind panic and uncontrollable fear. It was a question she'd waited and hoped for. Some security at last – a future without concern. But the question had not lived up to her romantic, Hollywood notion of the event. She'd felt none of the imagined spasms of pleasure, intimate warmth and certainty. What she felt was intoxicating anxiety, panic and doubt. Throughout that first long, dawn hour she had curled up motionless on the couch, the cat fussing her for food, her mind in turmoil. She could hear his deep breathing in the room next door, oblivious to her turmoil, in a world far from her, private and distant. The cat pawed her face, its mouth slightly apart, purring loud.

Breakfast had been polite – functional. 'More coffee?' 'Another piece of toast?' He failed to mention the cold space he'd woken to. He'd stretched out for her and found her gone. The quiet between them at breakfast complete and unmentioned.

'I'm going for a walk', She'd declared bravely.

It was a glorious morning – bright – calm – at odds with her mood. Isolated and anonymous, she walked briskly and confidently, heading nowhere purposefully. Around her the world was happy. Fathers pushed buggies, keen to indulge their wives, smiling and protective. Some jogged pass – those persistent all-weather women, pushed by some unknown force to plod relentlessly, each footfall closer to the unachievable – the distance – the time. Some new converts, ten hours in, their trainers pristine, unhinged breasts bouncing deliriously, beginning their ten-minute smug slog.

Mina saw nothing other than the path she followed rigidly along the riverbank. She walked upright obediently, head held high, lips pouting, her head exploding with decisions that had to be made. Her feet didn't deviate, one at a time in a rhythmic and straight line, others manoeuvring around her, stepping out of the way.

It was then that she saw them. Their heads almost touching, conspirators smiling, oblivious to the movement and chatter around them. She felt nauseous, tried to swallow and was consumed by a burning heat in her throat. She watched the light breeze ripple his soft hair and the weak sunlight spattering off their prosecco glasses as they tapped them together. She stared at him, willing him to turn. But he continued, deep in conversation, oblivious to the world as he gently lifted a discarded piece of strawberry blonde hair out of her eyes and smiled at her.

At that moment Mina was resigned to her fate, to what she must do. She thought of the previous Mina, the empress majestically carrying her hat, assured, confident and decisive. She would find her again. She would hunt her down, search for her, reclaim her prize that was still in her grasp. She lifted her head high, quickened her step and stared doggedly at her newly resolved future, just as Daniel caught sight of her in the crowd.

31 WEDDING PLANS

February was a solemn and lonely month. The daylight hours were short, and Mina spent most of them alone, curled up on the sofa with the cat and her own thoughts, rolling her new ring nonchalantly around her finger. He lavished attention during the brief and sporadic moments he was home and in those sparse times, she felt loved and admired.

Her mother of course had been pleased, a triumph of normality. Her difficult and headstrong daughter was finally to be tamed by the mediocrity of married life. She bustled and made lists, fonts for the invites, relatives to inform, outfits to discard.

'Let's just run away and get married, shall we?' She'd said one evening, intoxicated by the misery of an hour-long rant by her mother over the importance of appropriate stationary. 'Let's just fly somewhere…go to your house in Greece – a small church – some tapas at a taverna'. She looked across at him, pleading, noticing for the first time that his nose seemed to be disproportionately large, the skin under his eyes dark.

'Mina. I want to do it properly for you. Let the

world know how much you mean to me. Let me do that for you'.

Initially, she'd felt there was purpose to the activity. Wedding planners to visit, shades and flowers to choose, gowns to try and menus to decipher. Nicole, initially reticent and verbally scornful had gradually become excited at the prospect of helping Alec to squander his money on lavish plans. The list of chores needing attention was endless and Mina quickly came to resent the entire fiasco.

She watched him, quietly working at his desk, a self-possessed smile invading his face.

'Doesn't the world already know we're in love? Isn't it obvious?' She studied his expression, noted that he was listening and added, 'I mean, it's meant to be about us, not what my mother wants.'

'Mina?'

'Yes?' She tried to hide the frustration she felt by his nonchalant and relaxed attitude.

'What are you saying about your mother?'

'Alec. Are you listening to what I am saying?'

'Of course,' He smiled warmly, winking at her playfully, 'You want to run away to get married.'

'After that?'

'Sorry my darling, I must just send this stuff by close of play today - why don't we talk about it later, over dinner?' He dismissed her with his smile, and she obediently turned and resigned herself to the exhibition of her wedding.

Lying absent-mindedly on his bed, their bed, she folded her grievances neatly into little boxes and sealed them tightly shut. Her world seemed quiet, vague, resigned. While those around her, busied themselves, pushing and pulling her towards her big day, Mina's pertinent anxiety grew. She knew that this was the right thing to do. She loved him, he loved her. They enjoyed each other's company. The sex was incredible. He treated her like a princess. She ran through the list again and again. It was all just perfect. Her eyes drifted to the hat box sat in the wardrobe, its soft texture and symmetry. She thought about that first meeting at Lucy and Simon's wedding. How she had felt sat between them. How the hat had hidden her fears, masked her insecurities. She moved her fingers delicately over the skin of her belly, feeling the gradual goosebumps rise and thought of the tiny collection of letters nestled deeply within the confines of the hat. It had been a long time since she'd permitted herself to undo the ribbon tie and re-read his letters. It had been a long time since she'd felt her heart quicken at the mention of his name.

32 THE RESOLVE

Daniel had heard about the impending wedding of course...who hadn't? Hunched over his laptop he punched the keys aggressively, sending banal pointless messages in response to banal pointless questions. His boss had been nonchalant but understanding; a couple of months working from home in London rather than New York while he continued to sort out 'family issues'. His sister had been jubilant, a big brother home to roost for a while rather than globetrotting around the world. For his part, the arrangement was proving less successful. Lodging in the spare room at his sister's house, surrounded by her loitering student friends had made working difficult, so he spent most of his time renting WIFI by the hour and buying expensive coffees in upmarket cafes. Daily deadlines had to be kept and his work patterns became evermore sporadic and stressed. His spacious loft apartment and evenings out with friends and colleagues in Brooklyn, seemed a long way away from the reality of life in North London in a Victorian student house. He could cope with the messiness and the cold (his sister rarely put the heating on). He could even cope with the constant shutting of doors as people moved around the house. What he found profoundly annoying was the loitering, the inert bodies, smelling faintly of dope and coffee, lounging on every available piece of furniture, talking incessantly about nothing. Sloth-like individuals' limbs thrown about paralysed by the belief that inertness was somehow 'edgy' and that movement was 'fucking old'. In that case, he'd prefer to be 'fucking anything' as long as he knew his arms and legs still worked. Not that his sister's friends didn't make him feel welcome. This was part of the problem. Their incessant need to include him in conversation – to refer questions to him – to pick his brain.

'What do you think Daniel?'

'About what?'

'About whether we should boycott Tesco?'

'Umm…not sure…your reasons for doing so?' I don't care, he silently screamed…does it really matter…what are you all talking about…

'Well, I suppose if you feel strongly that it is affecting your local community in some way'.

'You see, I knew Daniel would agree'. No, you don't see, he thought, I just want you to stop discussing banal shite and let me focus on keeping my job and winning back Mina.

'So, is boycotting the way forward, or should we try something more passive-aggressive?'

'What do you think Daniel, about climate change?'

'What do you think Daniel about the American

obsession with guns?'

'What do you think Daniel?'

'I'm going out for a bit sis – have to make some calls. Don't let them coerce you into anything illegal'.

'Sure thing…we might be out when you get back…project that needs the help of the Natural History Museum'. Thank God he thought – some peace at last.

'Take care…I'll see you later.'

It was cold outside. The sky, school uniform grey, hung heavy and forlorn. Daniel wrapped his coat tight around his laptop and considered his next move. Since seeing Mina on New Year's Day, he'd become obsessed with finding opportunities to bump in to her – which in London wasn't a particularly fertile plan. Travelling aimlessly around the underground system to avoid his sister's house mates, was simply an excuse to be out there, where she was, in the world, the real world. Mutual friends would sometimes lower their voices when talking about her – a knowing look – an exchange of glances – the 'speak later' code of conduct shared facially amongst friends. What he knew was accurate information was that she was officially engaged to Alec Spencer, that they were planning a rather large and stylish wedding in the spring and that it was unlikely that he'd be invited. While he questioned the speed of both the engagement and the impending wedding plans, he didn't question his growing feelings that were becoming stronger every day. There had to be something he could do, some way he could get a sign to her – stop her from the potential calamity of this delusion, this decision and instead, come away with him. Yet, even as he said it, he realized this in itself was a fantasy, orchestrated by a lonely man in his early thirties who was cross that he had 'lost the girl'. What romantic banality. He could barely believe the ridiculous emotional explosion he was now inhabiting.

Cutting through the crowds he descended into the bowels of the tube and focused on looking purposeful, walking quickly down both escalators, tutting at those blocking his way and rushing headlong onto the platform, only to stand and wait the agonizing 2 minutes, 5 seconds until the next tube arrived. He'd been home almost eight weeks now and still there seemed no solution. Inside, he knew an urge was blistering, a desire to fly away festering, like so many times before. So, each day, he gave himself a limit. I'll stay until the weekend. I'll just have Sunday lunch with mum. I'll just finish that outstanding article. And as each week passed, his hope of rectifying the situation seemed to get further and further away. Part of the problem was there was no solution. He didn't have a plan. And by not having a plan, there were no discrete actions to take. Pride and anxiety prevented him from picking up the phone and his dismissive attitude gave no clues to his sister or friends of his inner turmoil. Standing with his head pressed against the tube door, he shoved his hand into his pocket and touched the curled edge of the envelope. He'd been carrying it around for weeks. An expression of his love and desperation, hastily written on New Year's Day, and rewritten and rewritten and rewritten. The final copy nothing like its original, it had sat in the envelope for several weeks, a discarded Christmas stamp stuck to the front and a dubious c/o address to her friend Nicole. Daily, it accompanied him on his travels, stroked and fondled, it lay nestled at the bottom of his winter coat pocket, crumpled and forlorn, waiting patiently to start on the next phase of its journey. Several times, Daniel had taken a lengthy diversion to a post office, determined to send his message and take the risk. But each time he was diverted by the thought of the inevitable, the rejection, the humiliation and the lonely flight home. Instead, stroking his hope, he carried it with him, a burning reminder, the possibility of another chance encounter – eye contact – embrace.

He pushed and shoved his way through the sweaty throng, up the escalator and out, the brittle cold air smacking his face hard. He stopped. His focus momentarily lost. He'd been here numerous times recently, ensnared by their one shared experience, caught in the anticipation of a brief encounter under the pretence of working in a creative space. Above the houses, he could see the looming industrial tips of the building piercing the chilled skyline. Once dirty and noisy, its cavernous interior was now filled with huge art installations, priceless pieces and swarms of people - none with the face he so desperately craved. He usually found a desolate corner, a peephole to watch from, one eye on his laptop, the other scanning the hundreds of faces, listening for her voice. Quiet in his solitude – he could be invisible – unquestioned – ignored. This was a place to while away an afternoon, attempt to work and stay vigilant. He stood contemplating, his breath short whispers in the cold, his hand clasping the envelope, his resolution to post it at the Tate firm.

Even the sun's loitering today, he thought as he stepped off the pavement straight into the path of a speeding taxi.

33 THE NEWS

Nicole was beside herself. No one would pick up the phone. She'd phoned both the home phone and the only mobile number she had. She had to let them know. It was their right. This was a real emergency, and no one would pick up the bloody phone. She could see her inner voice jumping up and down screeching. She breathed, put both phones on speaker and sat listening to the chorus of dial tones and answer phones. Who else knew? Bad news seemed to stick to her skin...crust over and leave her with the mess to deal with...a great big, oozing, sticky mess in this instance. She began to rehearse what she was going to say, over and over again, piecing together the events in her head, making sure that she understood each minute detail, each singular catastrophe.

'Oh, for goodness sake' She yelled, 'answer the bloody phone.'

'Hello?'

'Hi, it's Nicole...Mina's friend...you know'.

'Hello Nicole...you ok...I was just saying to dad the other day that we haven't seen you for a while…you ok?'

'I need you to sit down'. She could hear the quiet at the end of the phone.

'That sounds ominous…I am meant to be going out. Why sit?'

'Just sit…please'. Nicole breathed deeply, trying to stay calm, trying to appear less upset than she actually was.

'You're scaring me now…what's happened?'

'They've gone…disappeared…done it'. Nicole's rehearsed speech disappeared, lost in the panic she suddenly found herself floundering.

'Done what? Who? Nicole, you are scaring me – what's going on.' She sensed the fear in her voice.

Nicole looked at the decaying remains of some lilies she had treated herself to. Bent at the stem, they hung precariously over the edge, their pollen splattered rudely across the mantelpiece, the scent strong and unappealing.

'They've got married'. She said resolutely. – the truth feeling the best 'Married, you know…hitched…tied the knot…married! Mina and Alec.'

The scream lasted for a while – piercing - torn from somewhere deep and guttural. Finally, she could hear gasps and loud theatrical sobs, Labour-day moaning, followed by dripping noses and wiped snot.

'Are you okay?' The question ridiculous but expected. 'Shall I come round?' Pointless and ridiculous, she thought. 'I'll be there in twenty minutes', she said. Pointless and ridiculous but necessary to maintain Nicole's moral integrity and obsessive desire to escape this alien and high maintenance family.

34 THE RUNAWAYS

She wasn't quite sure how she'd managed to convince him, not even sure she had. As the wedding approached and the anxiety around them rose, Mina became quieter, calmer. She began to take a backseat, watching the proceedings from afar, observing with no opinion, disconnected. She nodded or shook her head, purely in relation to the looks on their faces rather than in answer to their questions. She was acquiescent in all matters, unashamedly 'going with the flow', a calm, cold flower in the hot chaos of the wedding plans. She'd caught him looking at her some days, his brow slightly furrowed, a perplexing expression on his face. Then the moment would pass, he'd smile, and the conversation would continue. Some days, she hid from the world, meandering through particular galleries, quietly sitting and staring at a picture, contemplating her own boredom, amongst the throngs. On others, she stayed in bed, so-called to read, then sleep, lovely warm comforting sleep and she'd wake to the sound of his voice coming through the front door, his annoyed expression as she fumbled to dress and embrace him.

Then a fortnight ago, he'd summoned her to dinner, a small Thai restaurant they'd frequented many times before. Intimate and friendly, they'd been squashed into a candlelit corner, knees forced together, elbows touching.

'So, I was thinking', He began. 'This whole wedding situation'.

'Would you like to see the wine menu sir?'

'Yes, thank you. You seem kind of unsure, reticent about it. Doubtful'

'I'm not doubtful about us...it just feels like it's kind of got away from me...you know?'

'It's difficult...pleasing everyone...your mother, mine, colleagues, friends. There are right ways of doing these things and then...' he tailed off. The waiter hovered as Alec scanned the list, annoyed at the interruption and pointed distractedly at his choice. 'I know these things take time and energy to organize properly...I thought you might have enjoyed it. You know...thrown yourself into the seating plans, dress design, decorations...' Mina raised her eyebrows and he looked away.

'Really? Does that sound like me? You know my experience of weddings...choosing a hat is one thing...arguing for weeks over a seating plan another. Besides, I just thought it was about me and you, not the creation of some pantomime.'

'Pantomime?' She looked away, hearing the hurt in his tone.

'Not pantomime as such. Just showy you know. Over the top...complicated'. There was a lull as the wine was poured, the waiter deliberating over the opening of the bottle, the offering to Alec, the acceptance and the further filling of both their glasses. Both Mina and Alec looked downwards, the waiter invading the conversation, both their hearts beating, wondering where the next sentence would lead them.

'Why don't we just go away and do it?' She looked up sharply. 'You know, just get married – go to my house in Greece – a couple of witnesses…'

'Are you serious?' She met his stare across the table and knew that he was. 'Just disappear…not tell anyone until after the event? Even my mother?' He nodded, faintly - feebly.

'Yes. If it'll make you happy…stop all these fears you seem to have.' He pushed an envelope across the table conspiratorially and while her fingertips touched the buff paper, she didn't dare open it. 'Go ahead. Look inside'.

'I don't want to.'

'Open it.' Sliding her fingers inside, she knew what she'd find. She pinched the thin paper.

'When?'

'We leave tomorrow afternoon. I've arranged the paperwork. You just need to agree to it.' She smiled, for the first time in days, a broad natural smile that lit her eyes and made him feel warm and back in control of their relationship, his world. 'It's settled then. Hope you like the dress I've bought you.'

She did. They'd stood together on a quiet bay, sounding out the vows quietly and with feeling – their eyes locked – a lump of emotion in both their throats, aware only of the gentle ripple of the sunset tide and the closeness of the housekeeper and her daughter – the only witnesses. Afterwards, they'd gone to the local taverna where they'd attempted to drink homemade wine and danced to the strumming of a local guitarist. Later, lying on their bed listening to the cicadas and buzz of biting insects, their breathing kept time, their bodies in tune with the unity of the celebration and mutual happiness. Mina felt at peace, resolved to this next phase in her life – the warmth of his naked body close and protective. It wasn't until a few sun-drenched days later that they both realised that they'd have to tell the rest of the world. By then, the views of others seemed a universe away from the cocoon they'd been living in.

35 BED WATCHING

Sophie sat next to his bed and watched the bleeping box intensely, straining to understand what each blip and alarm meant, jumping each time something unfamiliar happened. For three months she'd sat and watched his inert body, his face peaceful, asleep, tubes connected and distributed, helping him to breathe, to live. Her daily visits had become contemplative, part of her daily life, like washing, brushing her teeth, going to college. As each day rolled into the next, her patience grew. The initial horror at what had happened, the constant fear of losing him, had been replaced by the calmness of waiting. Friends and family did shifts. Her mother did the mornings, she a couple of hours each afternoon. Cards and messages arrived daily, along with 'favourite' tracks, visual and oral messages that they played over and over again. It was calm watching him…waiting. She had been reassured by his tests, comforted by the doctors' words, believing completely in his ability to one day wake up and tease her as he used to do. He was in there somewhere, sleeping…healing and she was adamant that he wouldn't be alone...wouldn't be frightened. As a little girl, she'd hated the frequent storms, the thunder particularly and he knew that, always slipping into her room with his duvet and curling up on the floor next to her bed so she wouldn't be alone. She would lie awake fitful and afraid, comforted by his gentle breathing next to her bed. Sometimes, she'd hold his hand as he slept, feel the warmth of his blood pumping diligently around his body. Now it was her turn. She didn't want him to be alone...wake alone.

She hadn't found the letter initially. His clothes, cut from him at the scene, bloodied and torn, had stayed thrust deep in a carrier bag, stored in the hospital bedside cabinet. It had taken her weeks to notice it. Then, as if to hasten his recovery, she'd decided to take them home, clean and store them. It was then that she found the envelope. Creased, speckled crimson with his blood and addressed to a woman she didn't know. Sophie's initial desire had been to open it, discover the contents, know. But she lost the courage to do so, deciding to ask him instead, when he woke, when he claimed back life. The letter, placed delicately on her desk for safe keeping, quietly succumbed to the keys, dust and junk mail accumulated over time.

Day after day, Sophie curled up in the unforgiving plastic hospital chair, legs covered in an itchy blanket. She quietly watched him and waited. She had no doubt that he would fight this solitude and inertia. His soul hostile, berating his body for its weakness, willing it to heal. Sophie quietly watched him and waited.

36 A FORGOTTEN TIME

She watched the coverage on TV, late at night when he'd gone to bed, clandestinely: festival porn for her eyes only. She scanned the crowds for a glimpse of the girl she'd been, sexy and mischievous, a future full of possibilities. She'd not been back in the five years they'd been married. The festival girls had given up asking her. But she couldn't resist watching it live, the surging evangelical congregations, swaying and singing loudly, flags flying, theatrical smoke and lights. She knew that that Mina was still alive deep inside her, compressed and contained, but still close to her heart. Life now was organized, civilized, Alec maintained and thoroughly tedious. She shopped. She spent hours preening, ensuring the expected figure and making sure that Alec wasn't disappointed. She waited. She sat in her comfort zone and mourned her sweltering classroom full of sweaty hormonal adolescents. Mourned her lack of work and limited friendships. Despised her hatha yoga classes, green tea and constant hunger. Vibrant, wonderful London had become a desolate and lonely island. She could hear his repetitive snoring and snorting, rising into pitched crescendos, rudely stopping and then repeating. She had no intention of joining him there. On the screen, the camera scanned the throng, pausing longer than necessary on a girl, a woman, perched comfortably on someone's shoulders. She swung her t-shirt like a lasso, herding the eyes of the audience, her bare breasts pert and full. Mina involuntarily smiled, excited, in awe of this woman's confidence and beauty. Her hand cupped her own breast, naked under her robe and she was immediately saddened by the confines she had constructed around herself. The set completed, the camera panned out, the roar of the crowd, not satiated, hungry for more – a unified swell of shared pleasure. A spontaneous repetition of the final bars of the last song filled the sky as the fireworks crackled and the stage went dark. The audience remained in the darkness, singing loudly, arms stretched upwards, mouth wide, a zealous congregation hungry for more. She found herself joining them, stood, legs slightly apart, arms outstretched, mouthing the meaningless words, her heart beating excitedly, warmth spreading throughout her body.

Mina crept silently to the fridge, each socked footprint stealthy and incongruous. She had become an expert at being unnoticed, ignored. She poured herself a large glass of sauvignon and stared at her handbag, the song still playing over and over in her head. She knew what was inside, throbbing to escape, treasures surreptitiously sealed in an envelope. One she'd kept all those years, loathe to discard it, tattered and softened, the words JFK hardly discernible anymore – the phone number unreadable though tattooed eternally in her head. Evidence of an indelible memory. The other, newer, though equally tatty, crimson splattered, words of passion inside. She stroked the designer leather, ran her finger lightly over the zip, refused to contemplate the possibilities. She gulped the glass down in one and like all good women, folded this yearning into a neat pile and stored it in the linen cupboard at the back of her soul. Here it remained, unadulterated, lavender scented and contained. Mina silently opened the bedroom door and slipped under the covers, expertly avoiding any contact with his skin. She lay patiently, waiting for the wine to enthrall her blood stream and send her into the unconsciousness she so desperately desired.

37 SEARCHING

He didn't regard himself as a stalker, just an interested by-stander, an observer, inquisitive like those reporters who photograph celebrities on nights out.

Initially, he'd used the web...scouring Face Book, google and the like...looking for proof of life. Each time he found it; his excitement mounted. Her face, her smile, that dark shiny hair. He carefully collected the images like a curator, pinning them delicately into a special portfolio in his phone. Accessible via various obscure passwords, and only opened at special times, these images felt rare and special. In them all, she looked happy, carefree, contented.

Gradually, he began to vary his journeys, just ever so slightly, nothing that would smack of physical stalking. He didn't want to see her. Was horrified at the thought of meeting her...just wanted to be in the vicinity...breathe the same air as her, traverse the same roads. Overtime, these detours grew longer, more pronounced, more determined. Then one day he had turned a corner and she was there - stood talking to some friends, laughing, her eyes on fire. She was animated, holding her friends' attention, making them laugh spontaneously. Her body was as he had remembered it, athletic and toned, relaxed and yet purposeful. That first time he had bolted, hidden, heart racing in case he had been spotted. When he got home, he had thrown up, shocked by the feeling of indescribable loss.

The next day, he travelled to his sister's new house in Brighton, adamant and determined to deny himself the pleasure of voyeurism. But he couldn't sustain it. The distance only fermented his desire to be back, to touch her, to smell her, to hear her speak. In desperation, he returned and resumed his observations. He succumbed to the growing realization that at some point he would have to have her or let her go.

38 BETRAYAL

Mina watched him talk, endless words spewing out of his mouth filling the void between them. She smiled and nodded, picking up the gist of his convoluted story about people she didn't know, events she hadn't witnessed, problems she didn't care about. This was being supportive. This was listening to your husband's cares…being a good wife. He paused briefly, and she managed to think of a relevant question to move him on to the next point of his rhetoric.

'So, what did X think about that?' He smiled, not looking at her and continued. She looked at his soft eyes, straining to see the man within, the boy he'd once been, the man with gems instead of eyes. But they were blank, unseeing. She realized he wasn't talking to her at all, merely talking aloud, filling the atmosphere with his voice. This had begun an hour ago and here she was, still waiting for a 'how was your day'…'how did the meeting with X go?'…'What did it feel like seeing him again?' But she knew it wouldn't come. Just like she knew she needed to be patient and listen. After all, not to listen was unsupportive and as she'd learnt, there are always plenty of other women who will listen, who will gaze longingly at you as you meander through each tedious, banal story about themselves, before they are taken to bed and fucked for their patience. She felt her stomach tighten and tried to forget the text message she'd found – the vomit she'd thrown on to the curb – the anger she'd felt towards her not him. 'You can't have him' she'd screamed into the night air. 'I can learn to be patient too.' And she had. He'd sobbed about the mistake he had made, how it had 'happened' like an apparition or a 'sighting', how it meant nothing, how he felt she wasn't supportive of him and his work.

'You can't have him,' she'd yelled in her head to the unknown woman. 'I'm sorry,' she'd said to him, nestling her head submissively into his lap, 'I am so sorry I haven't been supportive enough, sorry, sorry, sorry, sorry, sorry. She accepted his weak caresses and began to hate him.

She was constantly on her guard then. Constantly made up and raunchy. Constantly striving to be thoughtful and interested, supportive and willing to listen. She became what he wanted her to be: the mistress on constant duty. Gone were the weekends relaxing in joggers or the evenings slumped in front of the TV. Those women don't survive marriage. Instead, she was attentive to his needs, beholden to his whims, suspicious of his every move. Every time he was an hour late, forgetful of an appointment or confused by his day, a piece of her died inside. Her heart didn't break – no jagged line down through the middle – no sudden explosion. Initially, it swelled, huge and throbbing; overcome with relief that he'd stayed, watching his every movement, desperate for any sign of affection or kindness. He was relieved, she could tell, but his behaviour didn't change. He showed no remorse. He became angry if she mentioned his 'indiscretion' (his words), wanted the status quo. Sex became more regular. She indulged his every whim, encouraged to keep him through her seductive skills. Now he violently turned his head away when she tried to kiss him during sex, refusing her pleas to be kissed. She allowed him to use her for his sexual gratification, fuck her hard for fucking's sake. Accepted his physical roughness. Strangled the part of her that desperately wanted his affection rather than his cock. More and more she watched him from afar – physically close but emotionally distant – shocked by his aura of self-righteousness.

His coldness and disregard physically hurt, a stabbing pain in her chest, deep and penetrating and she began to notice that each day his comments, his criticisms grew. She inwardly flinched over every filthy look, every blank gaze, every put down. Some days there were whole lists of things she had done wrong, attributes about her character he'd initially loved and now loathed. Condescending comments about the way she behaved, the things she believed in and the things she did. She outwardly apologized for all the perceived errors, which kept him firmly on his pedestal and her in his marriage. But each time she uttered the words, 'I'm sorry', 'I know I am', 'I will try harder' a little part of her hardened and she had to look away so he wouldn't see her expression and the self-loathing she was beginning to feel.

She cried a lot, privately and publicly; big, pillow-biting sobs and guttural moaning. A stranger would smile at her, and tears would well, a friend would comment that she looked 'tired' and she'd burst into lip dribbling. Friends started to comment about the 'old Mina', the feisty creature, swelling with confidence and assurance. Could she not find her way back? Their concerned phone calls became less. They were tiring of her drama, bored with what had initially been a tale of adultery and betrayal and was now merely time-consuming and somewhat irritating.

Then today, the whole shell had dissolved, melted; the flesh bursting through, a tingle of emotion that was warm and consuming. For the first time in many months, she'd realised that underneath the survival shell, she was still there - inside – the empress ablaze with optimism, courage and brimming with love. Just not for him.

She continued to smile in his direction, nodded appropriately at key points, listened attentively, and planned her escape.

39 A DANGEROUS LIAISON

Mina sat uncomfortably on the bar stool, conscious of her stocking tops that were digging uncomfortably into her pink thighs. The cavernous hotel reception area was clinical and busy. Neat lines of businessmen and foreign tourists checked in and out methodically, the receptionists stumbling over their limited English. The hotel bar, simply an extension of the foyer, included some scattered tables and chairs and a bar area, decorated ornately as a tourist's perception of a London pub. Her phone bleeped. Nicole. 'Has he arrived yet? ☺'

'No…going to go'. Mina turned her phone face down so she wouldn't see the return message. She had no idea what she was doing in a central London hotel on a Tuesday night, waiting for a man she hadn't seen for almost six years. She needed to leave, go now before she embarrassed herself.

'Stay. Deep breath. Nothing to lose ☺' She must talk to Nicole about excessive use of smiley faces. Nothing to lose? Nothing to gain either, she thought. A solitary man stared across at her and she was conscious of her stilettos and tight black dress.

She suddenly felt ridiculous, like some cheap hooker. She shifted, crossing her legs in an attempt to look demure and forced herself to read mundane junk emails purposefully. She re-read his message, urgent and brief. *Mina…I need to see you…talk to you'*. She'd deliberately ignored it for weeks, months; wallowing instead in the unhappiness she wore daily. But then sat on the tube one evening scanning the pictures in the Standard, a short article about New York had caught her eye. Next to a picture of the Empire State Building was his name. Mina had caught her breath. As she pulled into her stop, she shoved the paper down into her shopping. Later, alone in the flat, she had carefully cut it out, folded it precisely and slipped it inside the crimson scarred envelope. A week later, here she was, sat coquettishly on a stool, feeling above all apprehensive, something she hadn't felt for a very long time. The bar tender topped up her glass and passed a glass bowl of peanuts. Turning over her phone, she saw the trail of messages of encouragement from Nicole. Clearly, she was enjoying her friend's secret rendezvous while her new baby slept. Barely recognizable music competed with the throng of visitors. The lone man winked confidently at her, and she grabbed her bag to leave.

'Hey'. Mina felt his hand lightly on her shoulder and turned. She didn't recognize him at first, the crisscross of scars across his right cheek. 'Hey'. He smiled, and she stood transfixed by him, those same dark eyes, slight laughter lines in the corner.

'Drink?' He questioned.

'Yes. Please.'

The barman placed another mat and glass, returning with a bottle which he carefully poured. Daniel placed the room key between them, the plastic card oozing guilt long before it had been earned. She looked at him, at his eyes, his hands, the small curve at the small of his neck.

'You look beautiful.' She smiled then, caught off guard, eyes brimming, excited. He seemed relaxed, poised, assured.

'I saw your article in The Standard'.

'Yep...do odd bits now and again...nothing routine. You teaching still?'

'Haven't for a while. Been busy.' Managing my husband's behaviour she thought, managing my own. 'Have been looking, you know online, couple of agencies.' He smiled at her. His hand rising unconsciously to shield the pronounced indentations on his face as he did so. Reaching over, her fingertips touched his hand, and she left them there momentarily.

'That's good'. She nodded, returned his smile. Their knees almost touching, static excitement running between them.

'You? Have you plenty of work?' He nodded, taking her straying hand away from his face and caressing it carefully between both his palms. Neither took their eyes from each other.

'Permanent contract...back with my old paper.' Mina knew that her heart was racing, her face flushed, physical signs of her abject fear of what she wanted to do. Reaching with her left hand, she teased the door card off the bar and stood. In a silent slow dance, her other hand remained in his and they walked towards the lifts.

Later, lying on the wrinkled sheets, the air con unit blowing out freezing air over their naked bodies, he told her about the accident, the coma, the rehab. They talked and talked. Outpourings of emotions and feelings, punctuated with laughter, kisses and fucking. Their limbs permanently entwined, caressed, examined and stroked. Finally, as the meagre winter sun began to peep through the window, they dressed quietly and straightened their creases. In the doorway, he pressed her hard against the wall, his face inches from hers, eyes intense.

'Let's not say goodbye', He said. And they didn't. As the lift doors opened, they stepped out into the foyer and walked purposefully in different directions. Neither looked back.

40 SAVING MINA

When the intercom buzzed, she didn't even jump, she'd been waiting for this moment for a long time. The cat, deaf and deep in sleep didn't move as she slid him from her lap and into the waiting travel basket. Alec's guttural noises briefly paused, a grunt, a pause of breath and then the snorting began again; slow, loud and methodical. Mina didn't breathe, moving silently towards the door, pausing only momentarily to capture one last look, a screen shot of the last five years. She slid her coat from the hook by the door and grabbed her handbag. She could feel her heart racing, terrified and enthralled at the same time. She closed the door softly behind her, a slight click but nothing more. The neon stairwell sprung alight, making her jump and she had to deepen her breath to maintain her resolve. The lights of the car outside were silently impatient, urging her to hasten her steps. Toe by toe, step by step she moved awkwardly down, frightened to wake anyone in the neighbouring apartments. Finally, she closed the heavy wood door behind her and began to breathe, large gulps of the brisk autumnal air.

Nicole nodded reassuringly as Mina placed the cat basket into the back and climbed into the front seat and they embraced firmly.

'Hey.'

'Hey'.

'All good?'

'Yep…he's asleep…wont wake for hours.'

'Mina? You sure?' Mina caught her gaze and they both knew. 'Everything's in the boot, including that bloody hat box! Honestly Mina – I'd have thought you would have donated that dusty hat to Oxfam by now.'

'Oi…come here'. Mina leant over and held her friend tight. 'Couldn't have done any of this without you.'

'Of course, you could. You are one of the strongest people I know…you just forget that sometimes. Besides, the cat strictly belongs to me, seeing as I have spent so many years feeding it.' Mina smiled. She felt a glow begin to dissolve throughout her body. She flicked on the radio and they both giggled as the Foo Fighters blasted 'The Best of You' out of both speakers.

'When do you start?'

'A week Monday. Bit nervous if I am honest. Been a while.'

'You'll be fine…more than fine'.

'Nicole. Thank you.' Nicole reached across and grabbed her friend's knee. Their eyes met, and both smiled as the car pulled away from Mina's world and began its journey.

Mina cradled her bag protectively on her lap.

Deep within, her crumpled, treasured ticket sat secure, smugly accompanied by a new one, its ink black and clear. Mina sighed deeply. 'It's the moon that keeps us safe in the dark...makes the tide ebb and flow...lights us home...inhabits our hearts so that they glow wise and free.' For nights the words had played intermittently in her comfort zone, repeatedly, nagging her consciousness until she knew. She knew she had a plan B. She had fought and fought, hot, sweaty, and uncomfortable. Then finally she knew what she had to do. Knew instinctively. Knew that she had known all along. Knew absolutely that a real plan B, is not to have a plan at all.

THE END

ACKNOWLEDGEMENT

I want to thank my partner Nigel, and my children Megan, Elliot and Ruby for their unwavering support, patience, and love. At no point did they ever doubt me or dampen my dreams.

HELEN ELIZABETH

Helen Elizabeth is a writer, a mother and an avid music fan who spends her days traversing the M4 between London and Bristol. By day, she writes educational policy. By night, she searches for adventure either in fiction or reality. She has raised three beautiful human beings who make her proud every day and one bonkers spaniel who often lets her day. Helen has a degree in English literature and a MA in education. This is her debut novel.

Printed in Great Britain
by Amazon

25778398R00106